CW01663088

OLD ENGLISH SPORTS

OLD ENGLISH SPORTS

Pastimes and Customs

BY

P. H. DITCHFIELD, M.A.

FELLOW OF THE ROYAL HISTORICAL SOCIETY; RECTOR OF BARKHAM, BERKS
HON. SEC. OF BERKS ARCHÆOLOGICAL SOCIETY
ETC.

Republished by
EP Publishing Limited
British Book Centre, Inc.
1975

Republished 1975 by EP Publishing Limited
East Ardsley, Wakefield
Yorkshire, England
and
British Book Centre, Inc.
996 Lexington Ave.,
New York, N.Y., U.S.A.
by kind permission of the copyright holders

First published by Methuen & Co., 1891

ISBN 0 7158 1044 8 (UK)
ISBN 0 8277 3272 4 (USA)

Please address all enquiries to EP Publishing Limited
(address as above)

Printed in Great Britain by
REDWOOD BURN LIMITED
Trowbridge & Esher

TO

Lady Russell

THIS BOOK IS DEDICATED WITH THE AUTHOR'S

KINDEST REGARDS.

PREFACE.

ENCOURAGED by the kind reception which his former book, *Our English Villages*, met with at the hands of both critics and the public, the author has ventured to reproduce in book-form another series of articles which have appeared during the past year in the pages of *The Parish Magazine*. He desires to express his thanks to Canon Erskine Clarke for kindly permitting him to reprint the articles, which have been expanded and in part rewritten. The Sports and Pastimes of England have had many chroniclers, both ancient and modern, amongst whom may be mentioned Strutt, Brand, Hone, Stow, and several others, to whose works the writer is indebted for much valuable information.

The object of this book is to describe, in simple language, the holiday festivals as they occurred in each month of the year; and the sports, games, pastimes, and customs associated with these rural feasts. It is hoped that such a description may not be without interest to our English villagers, and perhaps to others who love the study of the past. Possibly it may help forward the revival of the best features of old village life, and the restoration of some of those pleasing customs which Time has deprived us of. The writer is much indebted to Mr. E. R. R. Bindon for his very careful revision of the proof-sheets.

Barkham Rectory,
1891.

CONTENTS.

CHAPTER I.

JANUARY.

CHAPTER II.

FEBRUARY.

CHAPTER III.

MARCH.

CHAPTER IV.

APRIL.

CHAPTER V.

MAY.

OLD ENGLISH SPORTS.

CHAPTER I.

JANUARY.

> "Come then, come then, and let us bring
> Unto our pretty Twelfth-Tide King,
> Each one his several offering."
>
> HERRICK'S *Star Song*.

Dedication Festivals—New Year's Day—"Wassail"—Twelfth Night—"King of the Bean"—St. Distaff's Day—Plough Monday—Winter Games—Skating—Sword-dancing.

IN the old life of rural England few things are more interesting than the ancient sports and pastimes, the strange superstitions, and curious customs which existed in the times of our forefathers. We remember that our land once rejoiced in the name of "Merry England," and perhaps feel some regret that many of the outward signs of happiness have passed away from us, and that in striving to become a great and prosperous nation, we have ceased to be a genial, contented, and happy one. In these days new manners are ever pushing out the old. The restlessness of modern life has invaded the peaceful retirement of our villages, and railway trains and cheap excursions have killed the old games and simple amusements which delighted our ancestors in days of yore. The old traditions of the country-side are forgotten, and poor imitations of town manners have taken their place. Old social customs which added such diversity to the lives of the rustics two centuries ago have died out. Very few of the old village games and sports have survived. The village green, the source of so much innocent happiness, is no more; and with it has disappeared much of that innocent and light-hearted cheerfulness which brightened the hours of labour, and refreshed the spirit of the toiling rustic, when his daily task was done. Times have changed, and we have changed with them. We could not now revive many of the customs and diversions in which our fathers took delight. Serious and grave men no longer take pleasure in the playthings which pleased them when they were children; and our nation has become grave and serious, and likes not the simple joys which diversified the lives of our forefathers, and made England "merry."

Is it possible that we cannot restore some of these time-honoured customs? The sun shines as brightly now as ever it did on a May-day festival; the Christmas fire glows as in olden days. Let us try to revive the spirit which animated their festivals. Let us endeavour to realize how our village forefathers used to enjoy themselves, how they used to spend their holidays, and to picture to ourselves the scenes of social intercourse which once took place in our own hamlets. Every season of the year had its holiday customs and quaint manner of observance, some of them confined to particular counties, but many of them universally observed.

In the volume, recently published, which treated of the story and the antiquities of "Our English Villages," I pointed out that the Church was the centre of the life of the old village—not only of its religious life, but also of its secular every-day life. This is true also with regard to the amusements of the people. The festival of the saint, to whom the parish church was dedicated, was celebrated with much rejoicing. The annual fair was held on that day, when, after their business was ended, friends and neighbours met together and took part in some of the sports and pastimes which I shall try to describe. The other holidays of the year were generally regulated by the Church's calendar, the great festivals—Christmas, Easter, Ascension Day, Whit Sunday—being all duly observed. I propose to record in these pages the principal sports, pastimes, and customs which our forefathers delighted in during each month of the year, the accounts of which are not only amusing, but add to our historical knowledge, and help us to realize something of the old village life of rural England.

We will begin with New Year's Day.* It was an ancient Saxon custom to begin the year by sending presents to each other. On New Year's Eve the wassail bowl of spiced ale was carried round from house to house by the village maidens, who sang songs and wished every one "A Happy New Year." "Wassail" is an old Saxon word, meaning "Be in health." Rowena, the daughter of the Saxon king Hengist, offered a flowing bowl to the British king Vortigern, welcoming him with the words, "Lloured King Wassheil." In Devonshire and Sussex it was the custom to wassail the orchards; a troop of boys visited the orchards, and, encircling the apple-trees, they sang the words—

"Stand fast, bear well top,
Pray God send us a howling crop;
Every twig, apples big;
Every bough, apples enow;
Hats full, caps full,
Full quarter-sacks full."

Then the boys shouted in chorus, and rapped the trees with their sticks.

* Although the 1st of January was popularly regarded as the beginning of the year from early times, it was not until 1752 A.D. that the legal commencement of the year was changed from March 25th to the former date.

The custom of giving presents on New Year's Day is as old as the time of the Romans, who attached superstitious importance to it, and thought the gifts brought them a lucky year. Our Christian forefathers retained the pleasant custom when its superstitious origin was long forgotten. Fathers and mothers used to delight each other and their little ones by their mutual gifts; the masters gave presents to their servants, and with "march-paynes, tarts, and custards great," they celebrated the advent of the new year. Oranges stuck with cloves, or a fat capon, were some of the usual forms of New Year's gifts.

The "bringing-in" of the new year is a time-honoured custom; which duty is performed by the first person who enters the house after the old year has expired. In the North of England this important person must be a dark man, otherwise superstitious folk believe that ill-luck would befall the household. In other parts of England a light-complexioned man is considered a more favourable harbinger of good fortune.

The Christmas holidays extended over twelve days, which bring us to January 6th, the Feast of the Epiphany. It is stated that "in the days of King Alfred a law was made with regard to holidays, by virtue of which the twelve days after the Nativity of our Saviour were made festivals." Twelfth Day Eve was a great occasion among the rustics of England, and many curious customs are connected with it. In

Herefordshire the farmers and servants used to meet together in the evening and walk to a field of wheat. There they lighted twelve small fires and one large one,* and forming a circle round the huge bonfire, they raised a shout, which was answered from all the neighbouring fields and villages. At home the busy housewife was preparing a hearty supper for the men. After supper they adjourned to the ox-stalls, and the master stood in front of the finest of the oxen and pledged him in a curious toast; the company followed his example with all the other oxen, and then they returned to the house and found all the doors locked, and admittance sternly refused until they had sung some joyous songs.

In the south of Devonshire, on the eve of the Epiphany, the best-bearing trees in the orchard were encircled by the farmer and his labourers, who sang the following refrain—

"Here's to thee, old apple-tree,
Whence thou may'st bud, and whence thou may'st blow,
And whence thou may'st bear apples enow!
Hats full! caps full!
Bushel-bushel-sacks full,
And my pockets full too! Huzza!"

The returning company were not allowed to enter

* These fires signified our Saviour and the Twelve Apostles. One of the fires, which represented Judas, the traitor, was extinguished soon after it was lighted, and the materials of the fire kicked about.

the house until some one guessed what was on the spit, which savoury tit-bit was awarded to the man who first named it.

The youths of the village during the holidays had plenty of sport, outdoor and indoor, which kept out the cold by wholesome exercise and recreative games. Many a hard battle was fought with snow-balls, or with bat-and-ball on the ice; the barns were the scenes of many a wrestling match or exciting game at skittles; and in the evenings they played such romping games as blind-man's-buff, hunt the slipper, and others of a similar character. While the company sat round the yule-log blazing on the hearth, eating mince-pies, or plum porridge, and quaffing a bowl of well-spiced elder wine, the mummers would enter, decked out in ribands and strange dresses, execute their strange antics, and perform their curious play. So the wintry days passed until Twelfth Night, with its pleasing associations and mirthful customs.

Twelfth Night was a very popular festival, when honour was done to the memory of the Three Wise Men from the East, who were called the Three Kings. The election of kings and queens by beans was a very ancient custom. The farmer invited his friends and labourers to supper, and a huge plum-cake was brought in, containing a bean and a pea. The man who received the piece of cake containing the bean was called the King of the Bean, and received the honour of the company; and the pea conferred a like privilege on the lady who drew the favoured lot. The rest of the visitors assumed the rank of ministers of state or maids of honour. The festival was generally held in a large barn decorated with evergreens, and a large bough of mistletoe was not forgotten, which was often the source of much merriment. When the ceremony began, some one repeated the lines—

> "Now, now the mirth comes
> With the cake full of plums,
> When Bean is King of the Sport here.
> Beside, you must know,
> The Pea also
> Must revel as Queen of the Court here."

Then the cake was cut and distributed amid much laughter and merry shouts. The holders of the bean and pea were hailed as king and queen for the night, the band struck up some time-honoured melody, and a country dance followed which was ever carried on with much spirit. The king exercised his royal prerogative by choosing partners for the women, and the queen performed a like office for the men; and so they merrily played their parts till the hours grew late.

But the holidays were nearly over, and the time for resuming work had arrived. However, neither the women nor the men seemed to be in any hurry to begin. The day after Twelfth Day was humorously called St. Distaft's* Day, which was devoted to "partly work and partly play." Herrick, the recorder of many social customs, tells us that the ploughmen used to set on fire the flax which the maids used for spinning, and received pails of water on their heads for their mischief. The following Monday was called Plough Monday, when the labourers used to draw a plough decked with ribbons round the parish, and receive presents of money, favouring the spectators with sword-dancing and mumming. The rude procession of men, clad in clean smock-frocks, headed by the renowned "Bessy," who sang and rattled the money-box, accompanied by a strangely-dressed character called the Fool, attired in skins of various animals and having a long tail, threw life into the dreary scenery of winter, as the gaily-decked plough was drawn along the quiet country lanes from one village to another. The origin of Plough Monday dates back to pre-Reformation times, when societies of ploughmen called guilds used to keep lights burning upon the shrine of some saint, to invoke a blessing on their labour. The Reformation put out the lights, but it could not extinguish the festival.

In the long winter evenings the country folk amused themselves around their winter's fireside

* The distaff was the staff which held the flax or wool in spinning. All maidens were engaged in this occupation, and a "spinster" (*i. e.* one who spins) is still the legal term for an unmarried woman.

by telling old romantic stories of errant knights and fairies, goblins, witches, and the rest; or by reciting

> "Some merry fit
> Of Mayde Marran, or els of Robin Hood."

In the Tudor times there were plenty of winter games for those who could play them, amongst which we may mention chess, cards, dice, shovel-board, and many others.

And when the ponds and rivers were frozen, as early as the twelfth century the merry skaters used to glide over the smooth ice. Their skates were of a very primitive construction, and consisted of the leg-bones of animals tied under their feet by means of thongs. Neither were the skaters quite equal to cutting "threes" and "eights" upon the ice; they could only push themselves along by means of a pole with an iron spike at the end. But they used to charge each other after the manner of knights in a tournament, and use their poles for spears. An old writer says that "they pushed themselves along with such speed that they seemed to fly like a bird in the air, or as darts shot out from the engines of war." Some of the less adventurous youths were content with sliding, or driving each other forward on great pieces of ice. "Dancing with swords" was a favourite form of amusement among the young men of Northern nations, and in those parts of

England where the Norsemen and Danes settled, this graceful gymnastic custom long lingered.

DANCING ON THE VILLAGE GREEN.

The old country dances which used to delight our fathers seem to be vanishing. I have not seen for many years the village rustics "crossing hands" and going "down the middle," and tripping merrily to the tune of a fiddle; but perhaps they do so still.

In olden days the city maidens of London were often "dancing and tripping till moonlight" in the open air; and later on we read that on holidays, after evening prayer, while the youths exercised their wasters and bucklers, the maidens, "one of them playing on a timbrel, in sight of their masters and dames, used to dance for garlands hanged athwart the streets." Stow, the recorder of this custom, wisely adds, "which open pastimes in my youth, being now suppressed, worser practices within doors are to be feared." In some parts of England they still trip it gaily in the moonlight. A clergyman in Gloucestershire tried to establish a cricket club in his parish, but his efforts were all in vain; the young men preferred to dance together on the village green, and the more manly diversion had no charms for them. Dancing was never absent from our ancestors' festivities, and round the merry May-pole

> "Where the jocund swains
> Dance with the maidens to the bagpipe strains;"

or in the festal hall, adorned with evergreens and mistletoe, with tripping feet they passed the hours "till envious night commands them to be gone."

CHAPTER II.

FEBRUARY.

"Down with rosemary and bayes,
Down with the mistleto,
Instead of holly, now up-raise
The greener box, for show."

"The holly hitherto did sway;
Let box now domineere,
Untill the dancing Easter-day,
Or Easter's eve appeare."

Hunting—Candlemas Day—St. Blaize's Day—Shrove-tide—Football—Battledore and Shuttlecock—Cock-throwing.

THE fox-hounds often meet in our village during this cheerless month, and I am reminded by the red coats of the huntsmen, and by the sound of the cheerful horn, of the sportsmen of ancient days, who chased the wolf, hart, wild boar, and buck among these same woods and dales of England. All hearts love to hear the merry sound of the huntsman's horn, except perhaps that of the hunted fox or stag. The love of hunting seems ingrained in every Englishman, and whenever the horsemen appear in sight, or the "music" of the hounds is heard in the distance, the spade is laid aside, the ploughman leaves his team, the coachman his stables, the gardener his greenhouses, books are closed, and every one rushes away to see the sport. The squire, the farmers, and every one who by hook or by crook can procure a mount, join in the merry chase, for as an old poet sings—

> "The hunt is up, the hunt is up,
> Sing merrily we, the hunt is up;
> The birds they sing,
> The deer they fling:
> Hey, nony, nony-no:
> The hounds they cry,
> The hunters they fly,
> Hey trolilo, trolilo,
> The hunt is up."

We English folks come of a very sporting family. The ancient Britons were expert hunters, and lived chiefly on the prey which they killed. Our Saxon forefathers loved the chase, and in some very old Saxon pictures illustrating the occupations of each month we see the lord, attended by his huntsmen, chasing the wild boars in the woods and forests. The Saxon king, Edgar, imposed a tribute of wolves' heads, and Athelstan ordered the payment of fines in hawks and strong-scented dogs. Edward the Confessor, too, who scorned worldly amusements, used to take "delight in following a pack of swift dogs, and in cheering them with his voice." The illustration is taken from an old illumination which adorned an ancient MS., and represents some Saxons engaged in unearthing a fox.

HUNTING IN SAXON TIMES (from an ancient MS.).

When the Normans came to England great changes were made, and hunting—the favourite sport of the

Conqueror—was promoted with a total disregard of the welfare of the people. Whole villages and churches were pulled down in order to enlarge the royal forests, and any one who was rash enough to kill the king's deer would lose his life or his eyesight. It was not until the reign of Henry III. that this law was altered. William the Conqueror, who forbade the killing of deer and of boars, and who "loved the tall stags as though he were their father," greatly enlarged the New Forest, in Hampshire. Henry I. built a huge stone wall, seven miles in circumference, round his favourite park of Woodstock, near Oxford; and if any one wanted a favour from King John, a grant of privileges, or a new charter, he would have to pay for it in horses, hawks, or hounds. The Norman lords were as tyrannical in preserving their game as their king, and the people suffered greatly through the selfishness of their rulers. There is a curious MS. in the British Museum, called *The Craft of Hunting*, written by two followers of Edward II., which gives instructions with regard to the game to be hunted, the rules for blowing the horn, the dogs to be used in the chase, and so on. It is too long to quote, but I may mention that the animals to be hunted included the hare, hart, wolf, wild boar, buck, doe, fox ("which oft hath hard grace"), the martin-cat, roebuck, badger, polecat, and otter. Many of these animals have long since disappeared through the clearing of the old forests, or been exterminated on account of the mischief which they did. Our modern hunters do not enjoy quite such a variety of sport.

Otter-hunting, now very rare, was once a favourite sport among villagers who dwelt near a river. Isaac Walton, in his book called *The Complete Angler*, thus describes the animated scene: "Look! down at the bottom of the hill there, in the meadow, checkered with water-lilies and lady-smocks; there you may see what work they make; look! look! you may see all busy—men and dogs—dogs and men—all busy." At last the otter is found. Then barked the dogs, and shouted the men! Boatmen pursue the poor animal in the water. Horsemen dash into the river. The otter dives, and strives to escape; but all in vain her efforts, and she perishes by the teeth of the dogs or the huntsmen's spears.

Foreigners are always astonished at our love of sport and hunting, and our disregard of all danger in the pursuit of our favourite amusement, and one of our visitors tells the following story: "When the armies of Henry VIII. and Francis, King of France, were drawn up against each other, a fox got up, which was immediately pursued by the English. The 'varmint' ran straight for the French lines, but the Englishmen would not cease from the chase; the Frenchmen opposed them, and killed many of these adventurous gentlemen who for the moment forgot their warfare in the charms of the chase."

But I must proceed to mention other February

customs and sports. Great importance was attached to the Feast of the Purification, commonly called Candlemas Day (February 2nd), when consecrated candles were distributed and carried about in procession. At the Reformation this custom did not entirely disappear, for we find a proclamation of Henry VIII., in 1539 A.D., which orders that "on Candlemas Day it shall be declared that the bearing of candles is done in memory of Christ the spiritual light, whom Simeon did prophesy, as it is read in the Church on that day." Christmas decorations were removed from the houses; the holly, rosemary, bay, and mistletoe disappeared, to make room for sprigs of box, which remained until Easter brought in the yew. Our ancestors were very fond of bonfires, and on the 3rd of this month, St. Blaize's Day,* the red flames might be seen darting up from every hill-top. But why they should do this on that day is not evident, except that the good Bishop's name sounded something like *blaze*, and perhaps that was quite a sufficient reason! And why the day of St. Valentine should have been selected for the drawing lots for sweethearts, and for the sending affectionate greetings, is another mystery. St. Valentine was a priest and martyr in Italy in the third century, and had

* St. Blaize (or Blasius) was Bishop of Sebaste in Armenia, and was martyred 316 A.D. His flesh was torn with iron combs, so the wool-staplers have adopted him as their patron saint.

nothing to do with the popular commemoration of the day.

Now we come to the diversions of Shrove-tide,* which immediately precedes the Lenten Fast. The Monday before Ash Wednesday was called Collop Monday in the north, because slices of bacon (or collops) were the recognized dish for dinner. But on Tuesday the chief amusements began ; the bells were rung, pancakes tossed with great solemnity, and devoured with great satisfaction, as an old writer, who did not approve of so much feasting, tells us—

> "In every house are shouts and cries, and mirth and revel rout,
> And dainty tables spread, and all beset with guests about."

He further describes this old English carnival, which must have rivalled any that we read of on the Continent—

> "Some run about the streets attired like monks, and some like kings,
> Accompanied with pomp, and guard, and other stately things.
> Some like wild beasts do run abroad in skins that divers be
> Arrayed, and eke with loathsome shapes, that dreadful are to see,
> They counterfeit both bears and wolves, and lions fierce in sight,
> And raging bulls ; some play the cranes, with wings and stilts upright."

---

* *Shrove-tide* and *Shrove Tuesday* derive their names from the ancient practice of confessing one's sins on that day. *To be shriven*, or *shrove*, means to obtain absolution from one's sin.

But the great game for Shrove Tuesday was our time-honoured football, which has survived so many of the ancient pastimes of our land, and may be considered the oldest of all our English national sports. The play might not be quite so scientific as that played by our modern athletes, but, from the descriptions that have come down to us, it was no less vigorous. "After dinner" (says an old writer) "all the youths go into the fields to play at the ball. The ancient and worthy men of the city come forth on horseback to see the sport of the young men, and to take part of the pleasure in beholding their agility." There are some exciting descriptions of old football matches; and we read of some very fierce contests at Derby, which was renowned for the game. In the seventeenth century it was played in the streets of London, much to the annoyance of the inhabitants, who had to protect their windows with hurdles and bushes. At Bromfield, in Cumberland, the annual contest on Shrove Tuesday was keenly fought. Sides having been chosen, the football was thrown down in the churchyard, and the house of the captain of each side was the goal. Sometimes the distance was two or three miles, and each step was keenly disputed. He was a proud man at Bromfield who succeeded in reaching the goal with the ball, which he received as his guerdon. How the villagers used to talk over the exploits of the day, and recount their triumphs of former years with quite as much satisfaction as their ancestors enjoyed in relating their feats in the border wars!

The Scots were famous formerly, as they now are, for prowess in the game, and the account of the Shrove Tuesday match between the married and single men at Scone, in Perthshire, reads very like a description of a modern Rugby contest. At Inverness the women also played, the married against the unmarried, when the former were always victorious. King James I., who was a great patron of sports, did not approve of his son Henry being a football player. He wrote that a young man ought to have a "moderate practice of running, leaping, wrestling, fencing, dancing, and playing at the caitch, or tennis, bowls, archery, pall-mall, and riding; and in foul or stormy weather, cards and backgammon, dice, chess, and billiards," but football was too rough a game for his Majesty, and "meeter for laming than making able." Stubbs also speaks of it as a "bloody and murthering practice, rather than a fellowly sport or pastime." From the descriptions of the old games, it seems to have been very painful work for the shins, and there were no rules to prevent hacking and tripping in those days.

Football has never been the spoilt child of English pastimes, but has lived on in spite of royal proclamations and the protests of peace-loving citizens who objected to the noise, rough play, and other vagaries of the early votaries of the game. Edward II. and succeeding monarchs regarded it as a "useless and idle sport," which interfered with the practice of archery, and therefore ought to be shunned by all loyal subjects. The violence displayed at the matches is evident from the records which have come down to us, and from the opinions of several writers who condemn it severely. Free fights, broken limbs, and deaths often resulted from old football encounters; and when the games took place in the streets, lines of broken windows marked the progress of the players. "A bloody and murdering practice," "a devilish pastime," involving "beastly fury and extreme violence," the breaking of necks, arms, legs and backs—these were some of the descriptions of the football of olden times. The Puritans set their faces against it, and the sport languished for a long period as a general pastime. In some places it was still practised with unwonted vigour, but it was not until the second half of the present century that any revival took place. But football players have quickly made up for lost time; few villages do not possess their club, and our young men are ready to "Try it out at football by the shins," with quite as much readiness as the players in the good old days, although the play is generally less violent, and more scientific.

Hurling, too, was a fast and furious game, very similar to our game of hockey, and played with sticks and a ball. Two neighbouring parishes used to compete, and the object was to drive the ball from some central spot to one, or other, village. The contest was keen and exciting; a ball was driven backwards and forwards, over hills, dales, hedges, and ditches, through bushes, briars, mires, plashes, and rivers, until at length the wished-for goal was gained. Battledore and shuttlecock were favourite games for the girls, which they played singing quaint rhymes—

> "Great A, little A;
> This is pancake day!"

and the men also indulged in tip-cat, or billet.

There is one other custom, of a most barbarous and cruel description, which was practised on Shrove Tuesday by our forefathers, and which happily has perished,* and that was throwing at cocks or hens with sticks. The poor bird was tied by the leg, and its tormentors stood twenty-two yards distant and had three throws each for twopence, winning the bird if they could knock it down. The cock was trained beforehand to avoid the sticks, so as to win more money for its brutal master. Well might a learned foreigner remark, "The English eat a certain cake on Shrove Tuesday, upon which they immediately run mad, and kill their poor cocks." Cock-fighting was a favourite amusement on Shrove Tuesday, as well as at other times. This shameful and barbarous practice was continued until the eighteenth century; some of our kings took delight in it, and in the old grammar

* It was practised as late as the end of the last century.

schools in the North of England it was sanctioned by the masters, who received from their scholars a small tax called "cock-fight dues." Happily, with bull-baiting, bear-baiting, dog-fighting, and the like, this cruel and brutal pastime has ceased to exist. If we have lost some of the simple joys and cheerful light-heartedness of our forefathers, we have also happily lost some of their cruel disregard for the sufferings of animals, and abandoned such barbarous amusements as I have tried to describe. But the old sports of England were not all like these; the archery, running, leaping, wrestling, football, and other games in which our ancestors delighted, made the young men of England a manly and a sturdy race, and our nation mainly owes its greatness to the courage, manliness, and daring of her sons.

But Ash Wednesday has dawned, and all is still in town and village. The Shrove-tide feast is ended, and the days of fasting and of prayer have hushed the sounds of merriment and song.

CHAPTER III.

MARCH.

"And now a solemn fast we keep,
When earth wakes from her winter sleep."

"And he was clad in cote and hode of grene;
A shefe of pecocke arrowes bryght and shene
Under his belt he bare ful thriftely,
Well could he dresse his tackle yomanly;
His arrowes drouped not with fethers lowe,
And in hande he bare a myghty bówe."

Archery — Lent — "Mothering" Sunday — Palm Sunday — "Shere" Thursday—Watching the Sepulchre.

OF all the sports and pastimes of old England, archery was the most renowned, and many a hard-fought victory has been gained through the skill which our English archers acquired in the use of their famous bows. "Alas, alas for Scotland when English arrows fly!" was the sad lament of many a Highland clan, and Frenchmen often learnt to their cost the force of our bowmen's arms. The accounts of the fights of Creçy and Poitiers tell of the prowess of our archers;

and the skill which they acquired by practising at the

butts at home has gained many a victory. Archery was so useful in war that several royal proclamations were issued to encourage the sport, and in many parishes there were fields set apart for the men to practise. Although the sport has died out as a popular pastime, the old name, the butts, remains in many a town and village, recording the spot where our forefathers acquired their famous skill. The name is still retained in the neighbouring town of Reading, and in some old records I find that in 1549 a certain "Will'm Watlynton received xxxvi*s*. for making of the butts;" and there are several items of charges in other years for repairing and renewing the same.

Edward III. ordered "that every one strong in body, at leisure on holidays, should use in their recreation bows and arrows, and learn and exercise the art of shooting, forsaking such vain plays as throwing stones, handball, football, bandyball, or cock-fighting, which have no profit in them." Edward IV. ordered every Englishman, of whatever rank, to have a bow his own height always ready for use, and to instruct his children in the art. In every township the butts were ordered to be set up, and the people were required to shoot "up and down" every Sunday and feast-day, under penalty of one halfpenny.

The sport began to decline in the sixteenth century, in spite of royal proclamations and occasional revivals. Henry VIII. forbade the use of the cross-bow, lest it should interfere with the practice of the more ancient weapon, and many old writers lament over the decay of this famous pastime of old England, which, as

Bishop Latimer stated in one of his sermons, "is a goodly art, a wholesome kind of exercise, and much commended as physic."

The Finsbury archers had, in 1594, no less than one hundred and sixty-four targets in Finsbury Fields, set up on pillars with curious devices over them; but four years later Stow laments that "by reason of closing in of common grounds, our archers, for want of room to shoot abroad, creep into ordinary dicing-houses and bowling-alleys near home."

The famous Robin Hood, who lived in the reign of Richard I., was the king of archers. The exploits of this renowned outlaw and his merry men form the subject of many old ballads and romances, and the old oaks in Sherwood Forest could tell the tale of many an exciting chase after the king's deer, and of many a luckless traveller who had to pay dearly for the hospitality of Robin Hood and Little John. The ballads narrate that they could shoot an arrow a measured mile, but this is a flight of imagination which we can hardly follow!

"But he was an archer true and good,
And people called him Robin Hood;
Such archers as he and his men
Will England never see again."

Another ballad relates the prowess of William of Cloudslee, who scorned to shoot at an ordinary target, and cutting a hazel rod from a tree, he shot at it

CROSS-BOW SHOOTING AT THE BUTTS (from MS. dated 1496).

from twenty score paces, cleaving the rod in two.

Like William Tell of great renown, our English

archer could split an apple placed on his son's head at the distance of six score paces.

In time of war the archers were armed with a body-armour, the arms being left free. They had a long bow made of yew, a sheaf of arrows winged with gray goose-feathers, a sword, and small shield. Such was the appearance of the men who struck such terror among the knights and chivalry of France, and won many victories for England before the days of muskets and rifles.

We are now in the season of Lent, and our towns and villages were very still and quiet during these weeks. But there was an old custom on Refreshment* or Mid-Lent Sunday for people to visit their mother-church and make offerings on the altar. Hence probably arose the practice of "mothering," or going to visit parents on that day, and taking presents to them. Herrick alludes to this pleasant custom in the following lines—

> "I'll to thee a simnell bring,
> 'Gainst thou go'st a mothering;
> So that when she blesseth thee,
> Half that blessing thou'lt give me."

Many a mother's heart would rejoice to welcome to the old village home once again some fond youth or maiden who had gone to seek their fortunes in the

* So called from the Gospel of the day, which treats of the feeding of the five thousand.—*Cf.* Wheatley on Prayer-book.

town, and many happy recollections would long linger of "Mothering" Sunday. The cakes alluded to in the above verse, which children presented to their parents on these occasions, were called Simnells. In some parts of England—in Lancashire, Shropshire, and Herefordshire—these cakes are still eaten on Mid-Lent Sunday. Possibly they had some religious signification, for the Saxons were in habit of eating consecrated cakes at their festivals. The name Simnell is derived from a Latin word signifying fine flour, and not from the mythical persons, Simon and Nell, who are popularly supposed to have invented the cake. Hot cross buns are a relic of an ancient rite of the Saxons, who ate cakes in honour of the goddess of spring, and the early Christian missionaries strove to banish the heathen ideas associated with the cakes (which latter the people would not abandon) by putting a cross upon them.

In memory of our Lord's triumphal entry into Jerusalem, when the people took branches of palm-trees and scattered them in the way, on Palm Sunday our ancestors went in procession through the town or village, bearing branches of willow, yew, or box (as there were no palms growing in this country), which were subsequently carried to the church and offered at the altar. This custom lingered on after the Reformation, and until recent times the practice of going a-palming, or gathering branches of willow, on the Saturday before Palm Sunday, has continued.

Sometimes in mediæval times a wooden figure representing our Saviour riding upon an ass was drawn along by the crowds in the procession, and the people scattered their willow branches before the figure as it passed.

Thursday before Easter Day was called Shere, or Maundy, Thursday. The first name is derived from the ancient custom of *shering* the head and clipping the beard on that day; and Maundy is a corruption of the Latin word *mandatum*, which means "a command," and refers to the command of our Lord to imitate His example in the humility which He showed in washing the feet of His disciples. In memory of His lowly act the kings and queens of England used to wash the feet of a large number of poor men and women, and bestowed upon them gifts and money. This practice was continued until the reign of James II., and in our own day the Queen presents to a certain number of poor people bags of silver pennies, called Maundy money, which is coined for that special purpose.

Many of my readers are familiar with the rhyme concerning "Hot cross buns," but perhaps they are not acquainted with the superstition which our forefathers attached to them. A writer on Cornish customs says: "In some of our farmhouses the Good Friday cake may be seen hanging to the bacon-rack, slowly but surely diminishing, until the return of the season replaces it by a fresh one. It is of sovereign good in all manner of diseases that may afflict the family, or flocks and herds. I have seen a little of this cake grated into a warm mash for a sick cow." Hot cross buns were supposed to have great power in preserving friendship. If two friends broke a bun in half exactly at the cross, while standing within the church-doors on Good Friday morning before service, and saying the words—

"Half for you, and half for me,
Between us two good-will shall be. Amen,"

then, so long as they kept their halves, no quarrel would arise between them. In the West of England it was considered very sinful to work on Good Friday, and woe betide the luckless housewife who did her washing on that day, for one of the family, it was believed, would surely die before the end of the year. There are many other superstitions attached to the day, such as the preserving of eggs laid on Good Friday, which were supposed to have power to extinguish fire; the making of cramp-rings out of the handles of coffins, which rings were blessed by the King of England as he crept on his knees to the cross, and were supposed to be preservatives against cramp.

In old churchwardens' account-books we find such entries as the following—

"To the sextin for watching the sepulture two nyghts viii*d.*
"Paide to Roger Brock for watching of the sepulchre 8*d.*"

And as the nights were cold we find an additional item—

"Paid more to said Roger Brock for syses and colles, 3*d*."

These entries allude to the ancient custom of erecting on Good Friday a small building to represent the Holy Sepulchre, and setting a person to watch for two nights in remembrance of the soldiers watching the grave in which our Lord's Body was laid. At the dawning of the Easter morn the bells rang joyously, and all was life and animation. The sun itself was popularly supposed to dance with joy on the Feast of the Resurrection. But the manners and customs, sports and pastimes, which were associated with Easter, I will reserve for my next chapter.

CHAPTER IV.

APRIL.

"The spring clad all in gladness
Doth laugh at winter's sadness;
And to the bagpipe's sound
The nymphs tread out their ground.

"Fie then, why sit we musing,
Youth's sweet delight refusing;
Say dainty nymphs, and speak:
Shall we play barley-breake?"

Old Ballad (A.D. 1603).

Easter Customs—Pace Eggs—Handball in Churches—Sports confined to Special Localities—Stoolball and Barley-brake—Water Tournament—Quintain—Chester Sports—Hock-tide.

FROM the earliest days of Christianity Easter has always been celebrated with the greatest joy, and accounted the Queen of Festivals. Many curious customs are associated with this feast, some of which represented in a rude, primitive way the Resurrection of our Lord. There was an old Miracle Play which was performed at Easter; for we find in the churchwardens' books at Kingston-upon-Thames, in the reign of Henry VIII., certain expenses for "a skin of parchment and gunpowder for the play on Easter Day," for a player's coat, stage, and "other things belonging to the play."

Then there was the custom in the North of England of "lifting" or "heaving," which was originally designed to represent our Saviour's Resurrection. On Easter Monday the men used to lift the women, whom they met, thrice above their heads into the air, and the women responded on Easter Tuesday, and lifted the men. This custom prevailed also in North Wales, Warwickshire, and Shropshire.

The Pace Eggs, or *Pasche*, or *Paschal* Eggs, were originally intended to show forth the same truth, as the egg retaining the elements of future life was used as an emblem of the Resurrection. These Pace eggs were dyed, decorated with pretty devices, and presented by friends to each other. In the North of England, the home of so many of our old customs, the practice of giving Pace eggs still lingers on; and we find amongst the household expenses of King Edward I. an item of "four hundred and a half of eggs—eighteenpence," which were purchased on Easter Day. The prices current in the thirteenth century for eggs would scarcely be deemed sufficient by our modern poultry-keepers!

The decoration of churches and houses with flowers just risen from their winter sleep, the practice of always wearing some part of the dress new on Easter Day, all seem to have had their origin in the holy lessons which cluster round the festival of the resurrection. An old writer tells us that it was the custom in some churches for the clergy to play at handball at this season; even bishops and archbishops took part in the pastime; but why they should profane God's house in this way we are at a loss to discover. The reward of the victors was a tansy-cake, so called from the bitter herb tansy, which was supposed to be beneficial after eating so much fish during Lent. Of the various kinds of games with balls I propose to treat in another chapter.

At Easter there were numerous sports in vogue in different parts of the country. In olden times almost every county had its peculiar sport, which was regarded as a monopoly of that district. People did not work so hard in those days, and seem to have had more time and energy for ancient pastimes. Many of these old games have entirely vanished; others have left their old neighbourhoods, and received a hearty welcome all over the country. Berkshire and Somersetshire were the ancestral homes of cudgel-play, quarter-staff, and single-stick. Skating and pole-leaping were the characteristic sports of the fen country. Kent and Sussex were famous for their cricket; the northern counties for their football. Scotland rejoiced in golf, curling, and tossing the caber; while Cumberland and Westmoreland, Cornwall and Devon, were noted for their vigorous and active wrestlers. Curling, tossing the caber,* and wrestling have clung to their old homes; but the other sports have wandered far and wide, and are no longer confined to their native counties.

At Easter the local favourite sport was renewed with zest and eagerness, and almost everywhere foot-races were run, the prize of the conqueror being a tansy-cake. Stoolball and barley-brake were also favourite games in this month, as Poor Robin says in his *Almanack* for 1677. Barley-brake seems to have been a very merry game, in which the ladies took part, and of which we find some very bright descriptions in the writings of some old English poets. The only science of the pastime consisted in one couple trying with "waiting foot and watchful eye" to catch the others and bear them off as captives.

An old writer thus describes a water tournament, which seems to have been a popular pastime among the youths of London at Easter—"They fight battels on the water. A shield is hanged upon a pole (this is a kind of quintain) fixed in the midst of the stream. A boat is prepared without oars, to be carried by the violence of the water, and in the fore-part thereof standeth a young man ready to give

* The caber is a small tree, or beam, heavier at one end than the other. The performer holds this perpendicularly, with the smaller end downwards, and his object is to toss it so as to make it fall on the other end.

charge upon the shield with his lance. If so be he break his lance against the shield, and do not fall, he is thought to have performed a worthy deed. If so be that, without breaking his lance, he runneth strongly against the shield, down he falleth into the water, for the boat is violently tossed with the tide; but on each side of the shield ride two boats furnished with young men, which recover him that falleth as soon as they may. Upon the bridge, wharves, and houses by the river-side, stand great numbers to see and laugh thereat." Stow thus describes the water tournament—" I have seen also in the summer season, upon the river Thames, some rowed in wherries, with staves in their hands, flat at the fore-end, running one against the other; and for the most part, one or both of them were overthrown and well ducked." This sport on the water was a variety of the famous quintain, which was itself derived from the jousts or tournaments, only, instead of a human adversary, the knight or squire, riding on a horse, charged a shield or wooden figure attached to a piece of wood, which easily turned round upon the top of a post. At the other end of the wood was a heavy bag of sand, which, when the rider struck the shield with his lance, swung round and struck him with great force on the back if he did not ride fast and so escape his ponderous foe. There were other forms of this sport, which is so ancient that its origin has been lost in antiquity. Queen Elizabeth was very much amused at Kenilworth Castle by the hard knocks which the inexpert riders received from the rotating sand-bag when they charged "a comely quintane" in her royal presence in the year 1575.

A handsome quintain still stands on Offham village green, in Kent, although it is no longer used for the skilful practice of former days. It is the custom to hoist married men, who are not blest with children, on the quintain, which is made to revolve rapidly. Sometimes discontented and disobedient wives share the same fate.

Chester was famous for its Easter sports, when the mayor with his mace, the corporation with twenty guilds, marched to the Rood-eye, to play at football. But "inasmuch as great strife did arise among the young persons of the same city" on account of the game, a change was made in the reign of Henry VIII., and foot-races and horse-races were substituted for the time-honoured football, and an arrow of silver was given to the best archer.

But Easter sports are almost finished: however, we have not long to wait for another popular anniversary; for the famous Hock-tide sports always took place a fortnight after Easter, and much amusement, and profit also, were derived from the quaint observances of Hock Monday and Tuesday. The meaning of the word and the origin of the custom have been the subjects of much conjecture; but the festival is supposed to be held in remembrance of the victory of our Saxon forefathers over the Danes in the time of Ethelred. The custom was that on Hock Monday the men should go out into the streets and roads with cords, and stop and bind all the women they met, releasing them on payment of a small ransom. On the following day the women bound the men, and the proceeds were devoted to charitable purposes. It is to be noted that the women always extracted the most money, and in the old churchwardens' accounts we find frequent records of this strange method of collecting subscriptions—*e. g.*, St. Lawrence's, Reading, A.D. 1499 :—"Item, received of Hoc money gaderyd" (gathered) "of women xx*s*. Item, received of Hoc money gaderyd of men iiij*s*." We also find that the women had a supper given to them as a reward for their exertions, for there is the "item for wives' supper at Hock-tide xxiij*d*."

The observance of Hock-tide seems to have been particularly popular in the ancient town of Reading. At Coventry there was an "old Coventry Play of Hock Tuesday," which was performed with great delight before Queen Elizabeth at Kenilworth: the players divided themselves into two companies to represent the Saxons and the Danes: a great battle ensued, and by the help of the Saxon women the former were victorious, and led the Danes captive. The queen laughed much at the pageant, and gave the performers two bucks and five marks in money.

So ends the month of sunshine and of shower; but the rustic youths are making ready for the morris-dance, and the merry milk-maids are preparing their ribbons to adorn themselves for the revels of May Day. The May-pole is being erected on the village green, and all is in readiness for the rejoicings of to-morrow.

CHAPTER V.

MAY.

"Colin met Sylvia on the green
Once on the charming first of May,
And shepherds ne'er tell false, I ween,
Yet 'twas by chance, the shepherds say.

"Colin he bow'd and blush'd, then said,
'Will you, sweet maid, this first of May,
Begin the dance by Colin led,
To make this quite his holiday?'

"Sylvia replied, 'I ne'er from home
Yet ventur'd, till this first of May;
It is not fit for maids to roam,
And make a shepherd's holiday.'

"'It is most fit,' replied the youth,
'That Sylvia should this first of May
By me be taught that love and truth
Can make of life a holiday.'"—LADY CRAVEN.

May Day Festivities—May-pole—Morris-dancers—The Book of Sports—Bowling—Beating the Bounds—George Herbert's description of a Country Parson.

THE spring has dawned with all its brightness and beauty; the nightingale's song is heard, and all nature seems to rejoice in the sweet spring-time. Our forefathers delighted, too, in the advent of the bright month of

May, which the old poets used to compare to a maiden clothed in sunshine dancing to the music of birds and brooks; and May Day was the great rural festival of the year.

Long before the break of day, men and women, old and young, of all classes, used to assemble and hurry away to the woods and groves to gather the blooming hawthorn and spring flowers, and laden with their spoils returned when the sun rose, with merry shouts and horn-blowings, and adorned every door and window in the village. The poet Herrick sings of this pleasant beginning to the day's festivities. Addressing a maiden named Corinna, he says—

> "Come, my Corinna, come, and coming mark
> How each field turns a street, and each street a park,
> Made green and trimmed with trees; see how
> Devotion gives each house a bough
> Or branch; each porch, each door, ere this
> An ark, a tabernacle is
> Made up of white-thorn neatly interwove."

The men blew cow-horns to usher in the spring, and the maids carried garlands to hang them in the churches; while at Oxford the choristers of Magdalen College assemble at the top of the tower at early dawn, and sing hymns of thankfulness because spring has come again. This pleasing custom is still observed every year on the first of May.

But let us away to the village green, where the May-pole is being adorned with a few finishing touches, and is covered with flowers and ribbons. It has been carried here by twenty or thirty yoke of oxen, their horns decorated with sweet flowers, and then, with shouts and laughter, and with song, the young men raise the massive pole with handkerchiefs and flags streaming on the top, and the rustic feast and dance begin.

> "The May-pole is up,
> Now give me the cup,
> I'll drink to the garlands around it;
> But first unto those
> Whose hands did compose
> The glory of flowers that crown'd it." *

A company of morris-dancers approach, and a circle is made round the May-pole in which they can perform. First comes a man dressed in a green tunic, with a bow, arrows, and bugle-horn, who represents Robin Hood, and by his side, attended by some maidens, walks Maid Marian, the May Queen.† Will Stukeley, Little John, and other companions of the famous outlaw, are represented; and last, but not least, comes the hobby-horse—a man with a light wooden framework representing a horse about him, covered with trappings reaching to the ground, so as to prevent the man's feet from being seen. The hobby-horse careered about, pranced and curveted,

* *A Pleasant Grove of New Fancies*, 1637.

† Sometimes the May Queen did not consort with morris-dancers, but sat in solitary state under a canopy of boughs.

to the great amusement of the company. The morris-dancers are adorned with bells, which jingle merrily as they dance. But a formidable-looking dragon approaches, which hisses and flaps his wings, and looks very fierce, making the hobby-horse kick and rear frantically. When the animals have wearied themselves, the maidens dance again, and the archers set up their targets on the lower end of the green, where a close contest ensues, and after many shots the victor is crowned with a laurel wreath.

Such were some of the sights and sounds of May Day in olden times. But the Puritans, who slew their king, Charles I., were very much opposed to all joyousness and mirth, and one of their first acts when they came into power was to put down the May-pole. They ordered that all May-poles (which they called "a heathenish vanity, generally abused to superstition and wickedness") shall be taken down by the constables and churchwardens, and that the said officers be fined five shillings till the said May-poles be taken down. So the merry May songs were hushed for many a long year, until Charles II. was restored to his throne, and then the stately pole was reared once more, and Robin Hood and his merry crew began their sports again. But times change, and we change with them: customs pass away, and with them have long vanished the May-pole and its bright group of light-hearted rustics. An American writer who visited this country thus describes his feeling when he saw an old May-pole still standing at Chester—"I shall never forget my delight. My fancy adorned it with wreaths of flowers, and peopled the green bank with all the dancing revelry of May Day. I value every custom that tends to infuse poetical feeling into the common people, and to sweeten and soften the rudeness of rustic manners without destroying their simplicity. Indeed, it is to the decline of this happy simplicity that the decline of this custom may be traced, and the rural dance on the green, and the homely May-day pageant, have gradually disappeared in proportion as the peasantry have become expensive and artificial in their pleasures, and too knowing for simple enjoyment. Some attempts, indeed, have been made by men of both taste and learning to rally back the popular feeling to their standards of primitive simplicity; but the time has gone by, the feeling has become chilled by habits of gain and traffic, the country apes the manners and amusements of the town, and little is heard of May Day at present, except from the lamentations of authors, who sigh after it from among the brick walls of the city."

The name of the parish of St. Andrew *Undershaft* records the place where the city May-pole, or *shaft*, was erected, and *Shaft Alley* the place where it lay when it was not required for use.

The proclamation of James I., called the "Book of Sports," which was renewed by King Charles I., throws some light upon the sports in vogue during his reign. It was enacted "for his good people's lawful recreation, after the end of Divine service, that his good people be not disturbed, or discouraged, from any lawful recreation, such as dancing for men and women, archery for men, leaping, vaulting, or any such harmless recreations; nor from having May games, Whitsun ales, and morris dances, and the setting up of May-poles, and other sports therewith used, so as the same be had in due and convenient time, without impediment or neglect of Divine service. And that women shall have leave to carry rushes to the church for the decorating of it, according to their old custom. But withal his Majesty doth hereby account still as prohibited all unlawful games to be used on Sundays only, as bear and bull-baiting, interludes, and at all times in the meaner sort of people by law prohibited, bowling."

Why his Majesty should have been so very severe on the game of bowls, which is a very ancient pastime, and innocent enough, is not at first quite clear; but it appears that the numerous bowling-alleys in London were, in the sixteenth century, the resorts of very bad company, and the nests of gambling and vice. Hence the severity of King James' strictures on bowling.

The people of Lancashire in the time of James I. were as devoted to sports and amusement as they are now; and when the king was making a progress through Lancashire, "he received a petition from some servants, labourers, mechanics, and other vulgar persons, complaining that they were debarred from dancing, playing, church-ales—in a word, from all recreations on Sundays after Divine service." King James hated Puritanism and loved recreation ; so he readily granted the petition of the Lancashire folk, and issued a proclamation encouraging Sunday pastimes, which is known as the famous "Book of Sports."

In Ireland on May Day Bale-fires are lighted, and to this day young men jump through the flames, and children are passed across the embers, in order to secure them good luck during the coming year. On this day, too, the Irish kings are supposed to rise from their graves and gather together a ghostly army of rude warriors to fight for their country. The wild cries of the shadowy host, the clashing of shields, and the sound of drums are said to have been heard during the period of the last rebellion in Ireland.

On one of the Rogation Days, or on Ascension Day, it was the custom to go in procession round the boundaries of the parish to ask God's blessing on the fruits of the earth, and as there were few maps and divisions of land, to call to mind and pass on to the next generation the boundaries of the township or village. The choir sang hymns, and under certain trees, which were called Gospel Trees, the clergyman read the Gospel for the day, with a litany and prayers.

Sometimes boys were whipped, or bumped against trees, or thrown into a river, in order to impress upon them where the boundaries were. But they received a substantial recompense afterwards, and the whole company, when the procession was over, sat down to the perambulation dinner, and talked about their recollections of former days.

The advantages of this practice are set forth in George Herbert's description of a country parson. He says, "The country parson is a lover of old customs, if they be good and harmless. Particularly he loves procession, and maintains it, because there are contained in it four manifest advantages. 1. A blessing of God for the fruits of the earth. 2. Justice in the preservation of bounds. 3. Charity, in loving, walking, and neighbourly accompanying one another, with reconciling of differences at that time, if there be any. 4. Mercy, in relieving the poor by a liberal distribution and largess, which at that time is, or ought to be, used. Wherefore he exacts of all to be present at the perambulation, and those that withdraw and sever themselves from it he mislikes, and rebukes as uncharitable and unneighbourly; and if they will not reform, presents them" (*i. e.* to the bishop for censure).

This custom is still preserved, or has been revived, in many parishes, and at Oxford the boys may be seen on Ascension Day bearing white willow-wands, and beating the bounds of some of the old city parishes.

CHAPTER VI.

JUNE.

"The woods, or some near town
That is a neighbour to the bordering down,
Hath drawn them thither, 'bout some lusty sport,
Or spiced wassel-bowl, to which resort
All the young men and maids of many a cote,
Whilst the trim minstrell strikes his merry note."

FLETCHER, *The Faithful Shepherdess.*

Whitsuntide Sports—Church-ales—Church-house—Quarter-staff—Whistling and Jingling Matches—St. John's Eve—Wrestling.

AFTER May Day our villagers had not long to wait until the Whitsuntide holiday came round. This holiday was notorious for the "Church-ales," which were held at this season. These feasts were a means of raising money for charitable purposes. If the church needed a new roof, or some poor people were in sad straits, the villagers would decide to have a "Church-ale"; generally four times a year the feast was given, and always at Whitsuntide. The churchwardens bought, and received presents of, a large quantity of malt, which they brewed into beer, and sold to the company, and any inhabitant of the parish who did not attend had to pay a fine. Every one who was able contributed something to the entertainment. The feast was held in the church-house, a building which stood near the church. This was the scene of many social gatherings, and is thus described by an old writer—

> "In every parish was a church-house, to which belonged spits, crocks, and other utensils for dressing provisions. Here the housekeepers met. The young people were there, too, and had dancing, bowling, shooting at butts, &c., the ancients (*i.e.* the old folk) sitting gravely by and looking on. All things were civil, and without scandal. The church-ale is, doubtless, derived from the Agapai or Love Feasts, mentioned in the New Testament."

Whether the learned writer was right in his conjecture we cannot be quite certain, but church-ales subsequently degenerated into something quite different from New Testament injunctions, and were altogether prohibited on account of the excess to which they gave rise. Let us hope that all these feasts were not so bad as they were represented, and indeed in early times great reverence was attached to them, which prevented excess. The neighbours, too, would come in from the adjoining parishes and share the feast. An arbour of boughs was erected in the churchyard, called Robin Hood's Bower, where the maidens collected money for the "ales" in the same way which they employed at Hock-tide, and which was called "Hocking." The old books of St. Lawrence's Church, Reading (to which I have before referred), contain a record of this custom—"1505 A.D. Item. Received of the maidens' gathering at Whitsuntide by the tree at the church door, ij^{s}. vi^{d}." The morris-dancers and minstrels, the ballad-singers and players, were in great force on these occasions, and were entertained at the cost of the parish. In the churchwardens' account of St. Mary's, Reading, we find in the year 1557—

"Item—paid to Morris-dancers and the Minstrels, meat and drink at Whitsuntide—iii^{s}. iiii^{d}."

When the feasting had ended, archery, running races in sacks, grinning through a horse-collar (each competitor trying to make the most ludicrous grimaces), afforded amusement to the light-hearted spectators.

The game of quarter-staff is an old pastime which was a great favourite among the rustics of Berkshire. The quarter-staff is a tough piece of wood about eight feet long, which the player grasped in the middle with one hand, while with the other he kept a loose hold midway between the middle and one end. The object of the game was, to use the forcible language of the time, to "break the head" of the opponent. On the White Horse Hill, where Alfred fought against the Danes, and carved out on the hill-side the White

QUARTER-STAFF.

Horse as a memorial of his victory, many a rural sport has been played, and at the periodical "scourings of the Horse" many a Berkshire head broken to see who was the noted champion of the game. An old parishioner of mine, James of Sandhurst, was once the hero of quarter-staff in the early part of the century. The whistling match was not so dangerous a contest; the prize was conferred upon the whistler who could whistle clearest, and go through his tune while a clown, or merry-andrew, made laughable grimaces before him.

Another diversion common at these country gatherings was the jingling match. A large circle was inclosed with ropes, in which the players took their place. All were blindfolded with the exception of one, who was the jingler, and who carried a bell in each hand, which he was obliged to keep ringing. His object was to elude the pursuit of his blinded companions, and he won the prize if he was still free when the play ceased. It was an amusing sight to see the men trying to catch the active jingler, running into each other's arms, and catching every one but the right one. When the jingling match was over, a pig with a short, well-soaped tail was turned out for the people to run after, and he who could hold it by the tail without touching any other part obtained it for his pains. There was also a game called Pigeon-holes, which appears to have been somewhat similar to our present game of bagatelle.

And so with laughter and with song the feast ended, the evening shadows fell around, and the happy rustics retired to their humble thatched-roofed homes. The proceeds of these church-ales were often considerable. "There were no rates for the poor in my grandfather's time," says one writer, "the church-ale of Whitsuntide did the business"; and whether the parishioners had to pay a tax for the support of the King's army, or to repair the church, or to maintain some orphan children, it was generally found "that something still remained to cover the bottom of the purse."

Of the "mysteries," or miracle plays, as they were called, which were performed in towns on Corpus Christi Day and at other times, I propose to write in another chapter; and we will now proceed to the hill-sides near our villages on the eve of St. John's Day, when we should witness the lighting of large bonfires, and some curious customs connected with that ceremony. Both the old and the young people used to sally forth from the village to some neighbouring height, and there, amidst much laughter and with many a shout, they lighted the large bonfire. Then they danced round the blazing logs, and afterwards leaped through the flames, and at the close of the ceremony each person brought away with him a burning branch. This rite appears to have been a relic of Paganism. Probably the fire was originally lighted in honour of the sun, which our forefathers worshipped before they became Christians. The leaping through the flames had also a superstitious meaning, and the simple people thought that in this way they could ward off evil spirits and prevent sickness. The Roman shepherds used to leap through the Midsummer blaze in honour of Pales. The Scandinavians lit their bonfires in honour of their gods Odin and Thor, and the leaping through the flames reminds us of the worshippers of Baal and Moloch, who, as we read in the Bible, used to "pass their children through the fire" in awe of their cruel god. St. John's Day, or Midsummer Day (June 24th), was chosen because on that day the sun reaches its highest point in the zodiac. There is, however, another interpretation of the meaning of the fires on St. John's Day, as illustrating the verse which speaks of him "as a burning and a shining light" (St. John v. 35); but this interpretation was probably invented by some pious divine who endeavoured to attach a Christian meaning to an ancient heathen custom. The connection of the ceremony with the old worship of the sun is indisputable. Its practice was very general in nearly all European nations, and in not very remote times from Norway to the shores of the Mediterranean the glow of St. John's fires might have been seen. The Emperor Charlemagne in the ninth century forbade the custom as a heathen rite, but the Church endeavoured to win over the custom from its Pagan associations and to attach to it a Christian signification. In the island of Jersey the older inhabitants used to light fires under large iron pots full of water, in which they placed silver articles—as spoons, mugs, &c., and then knocked the silver against the iron with the idea of scaring away all evil spirits.* Sometimes bones were burnt in the fire, for we are told in a quaint homily on the Feast of St. John Baptist, that bones scared away the evil spirits in the air, since "wise clerks know well that dragons hate nothing more than the stink of burning bones, and therefore the country folk gather as many as they might find, and burned them; and so with the stench thereof they drove away the dragons, and so they were brought out of great disease."

In some most remote northern parts of England the farmer lights a wisp of straw, which he carries round his fields to protect them from the tare and darnel, the devil and witches. In some places they used to cover a wheel with straw, set it on fire, and roll it down a hill. A learned writer on antiquities tells us that the people imagined that all their ill-luck rolled away from them together with this burning wheel. All these customs are relics of the old fire and sun worship, to which our forefathers were addicted. Wrestling, running races, and dancing were afterwards practised by the villagers. Wrestling is a very ancient sport, and the men of Cornwall and Devon, of Westmoreland and Cumberland, were

* A Correspondence in *Athenæum*, Sept. 20, 1890.

famous for their skill. A "Cornish hug" is by no means a tender embrace. Sometimes the people bore back to their homes boughs of trees, with which they adorned their doors and windows. At Oxford the quadrangle of Magdalen College was decorated with boughs on St. John's Day, and a sermon preached from the stone pulpit in the corner of the quadrangle; this was meant to represent the preaching of St. John the Baptist in the wilderness.

At length the villagers, wearied with their exertions, retire to their cottage homes, marching in procession from the scene of their observances; and silence reigns o'er the village for a few short hours, till the sunlight summons them to their daily toil.

CHAPTER VII.

JULY.

"Swift o'er the mead with lightning speed
The bounding ball flies on;
And hark! the cries of victory rise
For the gallant team that's won."

Cricket—Club-ball—Trap-ball—Golf—Pall-mall—Tennis—Rush-bearing.

AT this time of the year all the cricket-clubs in town and village are very busy, and matches are being played everywhere. It may not therefore be inappropriate if I tell you in this chapter of the history of that game which has become so universally popular wherever our countrymen live. On the plains of India, in Australia (as some of our English cricketers have learnt to their cost), in Egypt, wherever Englishmen go, there cricket finds a home and a hearty welcome. But it is not nearly so ancient a game as others which I have already mentioned, although it had some fairly old parents, simple and humble-minded folk, who would have been greatly astonished to see the extraordinary development of their precocious offspring.

Kent and Sussex were the ancestral homes of cricket, which is thus described by an old writer—"A game most usual in Kent, with a cricket-ball bowled and struck with two cricket-bats between two wickets. The name is derived from the Saxon word *cryc*, baculus, a bat or staff; which also signifies fulcimentum, a support or prop, whence a cricket or little stool to sit upon. Cricket play among the Saxons was also called *stef-plege* (staff-play)."

I fear that our old writer must have made a great mistake if he imagined that the Saxons ever played cricket, and I believe that the word was not known before the sixteenth century. In the records of Guildford we find that a dispute arose about the enclosure of a piece of land in the time of Elizabeth; and in the suit that arose one John Derrick stated in his evidence that he knew the place well "for fifty years or more, and that when he was a scholar in the free school at Guildford he and several of his companions did run and play there at cricket and other plays." Also in Cotgrave's French Dictionary, published in 1611, the word *crosse* is translated "a cricket-staff, or the crooked-staff wherewith boys play at cricket."

In the eighteenth century allusions to the game become more frequent, although it was still a boy's game. It had its poet, who sang—

> "Hail, cricket, glorious, manly, British game,
> First of all sports, be first alike in fame."

It had its calumniators, who said that it "propagated

a spirit of idleness" in bad times, when people ought to work and not play, and that it encouraged gambling. But the game began to prosper, and several noted men, poets and illustrious statesmen, recall the pleasurable memories of their prowess with the bat and ball. In a book of songs called *Pills to purge Melancholy*, published in 1719, we find the verse—

"He was the prettiest fellow
At football or at cricket:
At hunting chase or nimble race
How featly he could prick it."

In the early part of the eighteenth century the game was in a very rudimentary condition, very different from the scientific pastime it has since become. There were only two wickets, a foot high and two feet apart, with one long bail at the top. Between the wickets there was a hole large enough to contain the ball, and when the batsman made a run, he had to place the end of his bat in this hole before the wicket-keeper could place the ball there, otherwise he would be "run out."

The bat, too, was a curved, crooked arrangement very different from our present weapon. The Hambledon Club, in Hampshire, which has produced some famous players, seems to have been mainly instrumental in reforming and improving the game. Its members introduced a limit to the width of the bat, viz., four and a quarter inches—the standard still in force—in order to prevent players, such as a hero from

Reigate, bringing bats as wide as the wicket. In 1775 they wisely introduced a middle stump, as they found the best balls harmlessly flying between the wide wickets. It was feared lest this alteration would shorten the game too much, but it does not seem to have had that effect, as in an All England match against the Hambledon Club, two years later, one Aylward scored 167 runs, and stayed in two whole days. England owes much to the old Club at Hambledon for the improvements which it wrought in the game, which has become our great national pastime.

Miss Mitford, in her charming book, *Our Village*, describes the rivalry which existed between the village elevens at the beginning of the nineteenth century, and gives a sketch of a match between two Berkshire village teams, which brought about some very happy results of a romantic nature. She tells us, too, of the comments of the rustics on the "new-fashioned" style of bowling which one of the team had introduced from London, which did not at all commend itself to them, but effectually took their wickets. When that celebrated company of cricketers, dressed in frock-coats and tall hats, whose portraits adorn many a pavilion, competed for the honour of All England, they were quite ignorant of "round-arm" bowling, which is, of course, an invention of modern times. Only "lobs," or "under-hands," were the order of the day. It has been stated that we are indebted to the ladies for the important discovery of the modern style of delivering the ball. The story may be legendary, but I have read somewhere that the elder Lillywhite used to practise cricket all through the winter, and that his daughters used to bowl to him. During the bitter cold of a winter's day they wore their shawls, and found it more convenient to bowl with extended arms than in the old method. Their balls so delivered used to puzzle their father, and often take his wicket; so he began to imitate them, and introduced his new method into matches, and thus the age of round-arm bowling was inaugurated. I cannot vouch for the truth of the story, and only tell it as it was told to me.* At any rate Lillywhite was the father of modern bowling, which would have startled and considerably puzzled the veteran cricketers in the early part of the present century.

The proper parent of cricket seems to have been club-ball, which is a very old game, and of which there is a picture in the Bodleian Library at Oxford, dated 1344 A.D. It represents a female throwing a ball to a man who is in the act of raising his bat to strike it. Behind the woman, at a little distance, appear several other figures of men and women waiting attentively to catch or stop the ball when hit by the batsman. There is a still more ancient picture of two club-ball players, representing the batsman holding the ball also and preparing to hit it, while the

* The same story is told of Willes, who is supposed by some cricketers to be the inventor of the modern style of delivery.

other player holds his hands in readiness to catch the ball. He has the appearance of a very careful fielder. Here we have the rudimentary idea of cricket; but how they scored their game, what rules they had, we cannot determine. Stool-ball claims also to be an ancestor of cricket, and consists in one player defending a stool with his hand from being hit by a ball bowled by another player. Here is a simple form of the modern game, the stool being used as a wicket, and the hand for a bat.

Trap-ball is a much older game than cricket, and can be traced to the beginning of the fourteenth century. The modern game differs little from that which the old pictures describe, except in the shape of the trap which holds the ball. But the most ancient of all games of this nature is golf, or goff (as it used to be spelt), which was played with a crooked club or staff, sometimes called a bandy. Scotsmen are very fond of this game, which has lately migrated into England and found many admirers. It was probably introduced into Scotland from Holland, and was a popular pastime as early as 1457. In spite of proclamations encouraging archery, and forbidding golf, it continued to flourish; it has a long list of royal patrons; and the Stuart monarchs seem to have been as enthusiastic over the game as all true golfers ought to be. Poets have sung the praises of golf, and the glory of the heroes who drove their balls along St. Andrew's Links, or those of East Neuk. The object

PALL-MALL.

of the game is to drive the ball into certain holes in the fewest number of strokes. James II. was an expert golfer, and had only one rival, an Edinburgh shoemaker, named Paterson.

If you have visited London you will probably have walked along the street called Pall Mall, which name is derived from an old game fashionable in the reign of Charles II. The merry monarch and his courtiers frequently amused themselves with this game, which somewhat resembled golf, and consisted in driving a ball by means of a mallet through an iron hoop suspended from the ground in the fewest blows. The game was played in St. James's Park, where the street which bears its name now runs.

Tennis also has a history. It commenced its career as hand-ball, the ball being driven backwards and forwards with the palm of the hand. Then the players used gloves, and afterwards bound cords round their hands to make the ball rebound more forcibly. Here we have the primitive idea of a racket. France seems to have been the original home of tennis, which in the thirteenth century was played in unenclosed spaces; but in the fourteenth it migrated to the towns, and walls enclosed the motions of the ball. In Paris alone there were said to be eighteen hundred tennis-courts. In the sixteenth century there were several covered tennis-courts in England, and some of our English monarchs were very devoted to the game. Henry VII. used to play tennis, and

PALL-MALL.

there is a record of his having lost twelvepence at tennis, and threepence for the loss of balls. Henry VIII. was also very fond of the game, and lost much money at wagers with certain Frenchmen; but, like

TENNIS.

a sensible man, "when he perceived their craft he eschewed their company, and let them go." He built the famous court at Hampton, which still remains. Charles II. also played tennis. The old game is very different from the modern lawn-tennis which is now so popular: it was always the game of the select few, and not of the many, like its precocious offspring; and there are only thirty-one tennis-courts in England at the present day. The court attached to the palace of the French King Louis XVI. at Versailles was the scene of some very exciting meetings in the early days of the French Revolution in 1789.

There were some other forms of ball-play, such as balloon-ball, stow-ball, &c.; but of these it is hardly needful for me to speak, as they are only varieties of those games which I have already described. The history of football has been narrated in a preceding chapter. You will be able to trace from the descriptions of these old sports the ancestors of our noble game of cricket, and wonder at the extraordinary development of so scientific a game from such rude and simple beginnings.

The floors of the houses and churches of old England consisted simply of the hard, dry earth, which the people covered with rushes; and once a year there was a great ceremony called "Rush-bearing," when the inhabitants of each village or town went in procession to the church to strew the floor with newly-cut rushes. The company went to a neighbouring marsh and cut the rushes, binding them in long bundles, and decorating them with ribands and flowers. Then a procession was formed, every one bearing a bundle of rushes; and with music, drums, and ringing of bells they marched to the church, and strewed the floor with their honoured burdens. Long after the rushes ceased to be used in churches the ceremony was continued, and I have witnessed a rush-bearing procession such as I have described. There was a rush-cart with a large pile of decorated rush-sheaves, and some characters from the May-day games were introduced. A queen sat under a canopy of rushes, a few morris-dancers performed their antics, and a jester amused the spectators with his quaint sayings. A village feast, followed by dancing round a May-pole, generally formed the conclusion of the day's festivities. In 1884 this pleasant custom was revived at Grasmere in the Lake district, when the children of the village carried out a "rush-bearing" after the manner of their forefathers, and the village green again resounded with songs of joy.

I fear that our ancestors were not always very cleanly people; they seldom washed their floors, and therefore they were obliged to adopt some device to hide their uncleanliness. The old rushes were not taken away before the new ones were brought in; hence the lowest layer became filthy, and one writer attributes the frequent pestilences which often broke out to the dirtiness of their floors and the masses of filthy rushes lying upon them. Perhaps some of the wise folks in Lancashire discovered this, for we find the following entry in the account books of Kirkham

Church, 1631—"Paid for carrying the rushes out of the Church in the sickness time, 5*s.* 0*d.*" Straw was used in winter: it would seem very strange to us to have our floors covered with straw, like a stable!

In this matter of cleanliness we have certainly improved upon the habits of our forefathers: dirty cottages are the exception, and not the rule, as they were in the days of "good Queen Bess"; and the absence of those terrible plagues which used to devastate our land in former times is due in a great measure to the improved cleanliness and more careful regard for sanitation by the people of England.

CHAPTER VIII.

AUGUST.

"Crowned with the ears of corn, now come,
And to the pipe sing harvest home.
Come forth, my lord, and see the cart
Dressed up with all the country art:
The horses, mares, and frisking fillies
Clad all in linen white as lilies.
The harvest swains and wenches bound
For joy, to see the hock-cart crowned,"

HERRICK'S *Hesperides.*

Lammas Day—St. Roch's Day—Harvest-home—"Ten-pounding"—Sheep-shearing—"Wakes"—Fairs.

THE harvest fields have begun to ripen, and the corn will soon be ready for the sickle; of this fact our forefathers were reminded by the Lammas Festival, which was celebrated on the first of this month. *Lammas* is a shortened form of the word Loaf-mass, or feast of the loaf. A loaf of bread was made of the first-ripe corn, and used in Holy Communion on this day; so this feast was a preliminary harvest thanksgiving festival

—a feast of "first-fruits," such as the Jews were commanded in the old Mosaic law to observe.

When the harvest was gathered in there were great festivities, and it has been thought that August 16th, St. Roch's Day, was generally observed as the harvest-home. St. Roch, or Roque, was a Frenchman, who lived in the early part of the fourteenth century, and was supposed to have performed miraculous cures, but August 16th seems to have been rather early in the year for a harvest-home. However, when the feast of ingathering did take place, there were great rejoicings in our English villages, and the mode of its celebration helped to knit together the masters and labourers, and to promote good feeling between them.

When the fields were almost cleared of the golden grain, the last few sheaves were decorated with flowers and ribbons, and brought home in a waggon, called the "Hock-cart," while the labourers, their wives and children, carrying green boughs, sheaves of wheat and rude flags, formed a glad procession. All the pipes and tabors in the village sounded, and shouts of laughter and of song were raised as the glad procession marched along. They sang—

"Harvest-home, harvest-home,
We have ploughed, we have sowed,
We have reaped, we have mowed,
We have brought home every load.
Hip, hip, hip, harvest-home!"

or, as they say in Berkshire—

"Whoop, whoop, whoop, harvest whoam!"

Sometimes the most comely maiden in the village was chosen as Harvest Queen, and placed upon her throne at the top of the sheaves in the hock-cart as it was drawn homewards to the farm.

HARVEST-HOME.

The rustics receive a hearty welcome at their master's house, where they find the fuelled chimney blazing wide, and the strong table groaning beneath the smoking sirloin—

"Mutton, veal,
And bacon, which makes full the meal,
With several dishes standing by,
As here a custard, there a pie,
And here all-tempting frumenty."

Frumenty, which is made of wheat boiled in milk, was a standing dish at every harvest supper. And then around the festive board old tales are told, well-known jests abound, and thanks given to the good farmer and his wife for their hospitality in some such homely rhymes as these—

"Here's a health to our master,
The lord of the feast;
God bless his endeavours,
And send him increase.

"May everything prosper
That he takes in hand,
For we be his servants,
And do his command."

The youths and maidens dance their country dances, as an old writer, who lived in the reign of Charles II., tells us :—"The lad and the lass will have no lead on their heels. O, 'tis the merry time wherein honest neighbours make good cheer, and God is glorified in His blessings on the earth." When the feast is over, the company retire to some near hillock, and make the welkin ring with their shouts, "Holla, holla, holla, largess!"—largess being the presents of money and good things which the farmer had bestowed.

Such was the harvest-home in the good old days—a joy and delight to both old and young. The toils of the labourers did not seem so hard and wearisome when they knew that the farmers had such a grateful sense of their good services; and if any one felt aggrieved or discontented, the mutual intercourse at the harvest-home, when all were equal, when all sat at the same table and conversed freely together, soon banished all ill-feeling, and promoted a sense of mutual trust, which is essential to the happiness and well-being of any community. Shorn of much of its merriment and quaint customs, the harvest-home still lingers on in some places; but modern habits and notions have deprived it of much of its old spirit and light-heartedness. We have our harvest thanksgiving services, which (thank God!) are observed in almost every village and hamlet. It is, of course, our first duty to thank God for the fruits of His bounty and love; but the harvest-home should not be forgotten. When labourers simply regard harvest-time as a season when they can earn a few shillings more than usual, and take no further interest in their work, or in the welfare of their master, all brightness vanishes from their industry: their minds become sordid and mercenary; and mutual trust, good-feeling, and fellowship cease to exist.

Neither did the harvest-men allow drunkenness, laziness, swearing, quarrelling, nor lying, to go unpunished. The labourers in Suffolk, if they found one of their number guilty, would hold a court-martial among themselves, lay the culprit down on his face, and an executioner would administer several hard blows with a shoe studded with hob-nails. This was called "ten-pounding," and must have been very effectual in checking any of the above delinquencies.

Besides the harvest-home there was also observed another feast of a similar character in the spring, when the sheep were shorn. A plentiful dinner was given by the farmer to the shearers and their friends, and a table was often set in the open village for the young people and children. Tusser, who wrote a book upon *Five Hundred Points of Husbandry*, did not forget the treats which ought to be given to the labourers, and alludes to the sheep-shearing festival in the following lines—

"Wife, make us a dinner; spare flesh, neither corn,
Make wafers and cakes, for our sheep must be shorn;
At sheep-shearing, neighbours none other things crave,
But good cheer and welcome like neighbours to have."

We have in many villages and towns a feast called "the Wakes," which is one of the oldest of our English festivals. The day of "the Wakes" is the festival of the Saint to whom the parish church is dedicated, and it is so called because, on the previous night, or vigil, the people used to watch, or "wake," in the church till the morning dawned. It was the custom for the inhabitants of the parish to keep open house on that day, and to entertain all their relations and friends who came to them from a distance. In early times the people used to make booths and tents with the boughs of trees near to the church, and were directed to celebrate the feast in them with thanksgiving and prayer. By degrees they began to forget their prayers, and remembered only the feasting, and other abuses crept in, so at last the "waking" on the eve of the festival was suppressed. But these primitive feasts were the origin of most of our fairs, which are generally held on the dedication festival of the parish church.* The neighbours from the adjoining villages used to attend the wakes, so the peddlers and hawkers came to find a market for their wares. Their stalls began to multiply, until at last an immense fair sprang into existence, which owed its origin entirely to the religious festival of "the wakes." Fairs have degenerated like many other good things, and we can hardly realize their vastness in the middle ages. The circuit of a fair sometimes was very great, and it would have been impossible in those days to carry on the trade of the country without them. The great Stourbridge Fair, near Cambridge, I have described in my former book on *English Villages.* The booths were planted in a cornfield, and the circuit of the fair, which was one of the largest in Europe, was over three miles. All kinds of sports were held on these occasions: plays, comedies, tragedies, bull-baiting, &c., and King James was very wroth with the undergraduates of Cambridge who would insist upon frequenting Stourbridge Fair rather than attend to their studies.

* The word *fair* is derived from the ecclesiastical term *feria*, a holiday.

The "Wakes," or village feast, was a great day for all sports and pastimes. A writer in the *Spectator* describes the "country wake" which he witnessed at Bath. The green was covered with a crowd of all ages and both sexes, decked out in holiday attire, and divided into several parties, "all of them endeavouring to show themselves in those exercises wherein they excelled." In one place there was a ring of cudgel-players, in another a football match, in another a ring of wrestlers. The prize for the men was a hat, and for the women, who had their own contests, a smock. Running and leaping also found a place in the programme. In Berkshire back-sword play and wrestling were the favourite amusements for vigorous youths, and men strove hard to win the honour of being champion and the prizes which were offered on the occasion. There were "cheap jacks," and endless booths containing all kinds of fairings, ribands, gingerbread cakes, and shows, with huge pictures hung outside of giants and wild Indians, pink-eyed ladies, live lions, and deformities of all kinds. There were minor sports, such as climbing the pole, jumping in sacks, rolling wheelbarrows blindfolded, donkey races, muzzling in a flour-tub, &c.; but the back-sword play was the chief and most serious part of the programme.

A good sound ash-stick with a large basket handle was the weapon used, very similar to, but heavier and shorter than an ordinary single-stick. The object is to "break the head" of the opponent—*i. e.* to cause blood to flow anywhere above the eyebrow. A slight blow will often accomplish this, so the game is not so savage as it appears to be. The play took place on a stage of rough planks about four feet high. Each player was armed with a stick, looping the fingers of his left hand in a handkerchief or strap, which he fastened round his left leg, measuring the length, so that when he drew it tight with his left elbow up he had a perfect guard for the left side of his head.* Guarding his head with the stick in his right hand, he advanced, and then the fight began; fast and furious came the blows, until at last a red streak on the temple of one of the combatants declared his defeat. The *Reading Mercury* of May 24, 1819, advertised the rural sports at Peppard, when the not very magnificent prize of eighteenpence was offered to every man who broke a head at cudgel-play, and a shilling to every one who had his head broken.

Such was the sport which our old Berkshire rustics delighted in. Back-sword play, wrestling, and other pastimes made them a hardy race, full of courage, and developed qualities which it is hoped their descendants have not altogether lost. The gallant Berkshire Regiment, which fought so bravely

* *Cf.* Govett's *King's Book of Sports*, and *Tom Brown's Schooldays*, to which I am indebted for the above accurate description of back-sword play.

at Maiwand, is composed of the sons of those who used to wield the back-sword on the Berkshire downs, and showed themselves not unworthy of their ancestry, although the quarter-staff and ashen-swords are forgotten. The old village feasts are forgotten too—more's the pity. Then old quarrels were healed, old bitternesses removed: aged friends met, and became young again in heart, as they revived old memories and sweet recollections of youthful days. Rich and poor, the squire and the farmer, the farmer and his labourers, all mingled together, class with class; and good-fellowship, harmony, and mutual confidence were promoted by these annual gatherings. It is true that these village feasts degenerated, because the well-to-do folk abstained from them; but would it not be possible to revive them, to preserve the good which they certainly did, and to eliminate the evil which is so often mingled with the good? Such a consideration is worthy of the attention of all who have the welfare of the people at heart.

CHAPTER IX.

SEPTEMBER.

"Nor is there hawk which mantleth her on pearch,
Whether high tow'ring or accoasting low,
But I the measure of her flight do search,
And all her prey, and all her diet know."—SPENSER.

Hawking—Michaelmas—Bull and Bear-baiting.

OF all old English sports hawking is one of the most ancient and the most fashionable. It has almost died out now, but there are one or two hawking enthusiasts who have endeavoured to revive this old English pastime, and on the Berkshire Downs a hawking party was seen a few years ago. Hawking consists in the training and flying of hawks for the purpose of catching other birds. Kings and noblemen, barons and ladies of feudal times, used to delight in following the sport on horseback, and to watch their favourite birds towering high to gain the upward flights in order to swoop down upon some heron, crane, or wild duck, and bear it to the ground.

Persons of high rank always carried their hawks with them wherever they went, and in old paintings the hawk upon the wrist of a portrait was the sign of noble birth. The sport was practised by our Saxon forefathers before the Normans came, and the first trained hawk in England is said to have been sent by St. Boniface, the "Apostle of the Germans," as a present to Ethelbert, King of Kent, in the eighth century. The history of the sport of the kings who loved to take part in it, and of their adventures, would require a volume, and my space only allows me to give you a brief account of the manner in which the sport was conducted.

I may mention that before the reign of King John only kings and noblemen were allowed to take part in hawking; but in the forest Charter, which that monarch was compelled to sign, every freeman was permitted to have his own hawks and falcons. The falconer, who took care of the hawks, was a very important person. The chief falconer of the King of France received four thousand florins a year, besides a tax upon every hawk sold in the kingdom. The Welsh princes assigned the fourth place of honour in their courts to this officer; but this proud distinction had its responsibilities, and this high official was only allowed to take three draughts from his horn, lest his brain should not be as clear as it ought to be, and the precious birds might be neglected.

Sometimes the hawking party went on foot, carrying long poles to enable them to jump the ditches and to follow the course. Henry VIII. nearly lost his life on one occasion through falling (his pole having broken) into a bog, from which he was rescued by one John Moody, who happened to see the accident. But mounted on gallant steeds the lords and ladies were accustomed to follow their favourite pastime, and amid the blowing of horns and laughter and shoutings they rode along, galloping up-hill and down-hill, with their eyes fixed upon the birds, which were battling or chasing each other high overhead. The hawk did not always win the fight: sometimes a crafty heron would turn his long bill upwards just as the hawk was descending upon him, and pierce his antagonist through the body.

Great skill and perseverance were required in training these birds. When they were not flying after their prey, they were hoodwinked, *i.e.* their heads were covered with caps, which were often finely embroidered. On their legs they had strings of leather, called *jesses*, with rings attached. When a hawk was being trained, a long thread was fastened to these rings to draw the bird back again, but when it was well educated, it would obey the voice of the falconer and return when it had performed its flight. It was necessary for the bird to know its master very intimately, so a devoted follower of the sport would always carry his hawk about with him, and the two were as inseparable as a Highland shepherd and his

A FALCONER.

dog. The sportsman would feed his bird and train it daily, and in an old book of directions he is advised "at night to go to the mews, and take it from its perch, and set it on his fist, and bear it all the night," in order to be ready for the morrow's sport.

The mews were the buildings where the hawks were kept when moulting, the word "mew" being a term used by falconers to signify to moult, or cast feathers; and the King's Mews, near Charing Cross, was the place where the royal hawks were kept. This place was afterwards enlarged, and converted into stables for horses; but the old name remained, and now most stables in London are called mews, although the word is derived from falconry, and the hawks have long since flown away.

The sport declined at the end of the seventeenth century, when shooting with guns became general, but our language has preserved some traces of this ancient pastime. When a person is blinded by deceit, he is said to be "hoodwinked," and this word is derived from the custom of placing a hood over the hawk's eyes before it was released from restraint.

On the Feast of St. Michael, or Michaelmas, the tenants were in the habit of bringing presents of a fat goose to their landlord, in order to make him kind and lenient in the matters of rent, repairs, and the renewal of leases, and the noble landlords used to entertain their tenants right royally in the great halls of their ancestral mansions, roast goose forming a standing dish of the repast. This is probably the origin of the custom which prevails at the present time of eating geese at Michaelmas.

When the harvest was over, and the farmers were not so busy, they often amused themselves by the cruel sport of baiting a bull. An old gentleman who lived at Wokingham was so fond of this savage pastime that he left in his will a sum of money for the purpose of providing every year two bulls to be baited for the amusement of the people of his native town. The bulls are still bought, but they are put to death in a more merciful manner, and the meat given to the poor. Amongst the hills in Yorkshire there is a small village, through which a brook runs, crossed by two bridges, and having a stone wall on each side. Thus, when the bridges were stopped up, there was formed a wall-encircled space, into which, once a year, at least, a poor bull was placed, to be worried to death by dogs, and within the memory of men now living this cruel sport has been carried on.

Nor was this only a sport for ignorant rustics; kings and noble courtiers, and even ladies, used to frequent the bear-gardens of the metropolis, and witness with delight the slaughter of bulls, and bears, and dogs. Erasmus tells us that in the reign of Henry VIII. "many herds of bears were maintained in this country for the purpose of baiting." Queen Elizabeth commanded bears, bulls, and the ape to be baited in her presence, and James I. was not averse to the sight. The following is a description of this barbarous entertainment—"There is a place built in the form of a theatre, which serves for baiting of bulls and bears. They are fastened behind, and then worried by great English bull-dogs; but not without risk to the dogs from the horns of the one and the teeth of the other." Even horses were sometimes baited, and sometimes asses. Evelyn, in his *Diary*, thus describes the strange sight—"June 16th, 1670. I went with some friends to the bear-garden, where was cock-fighting, dog-fighting, bear and bull-baiting, it being a famous day for all these butcherly sports, or rather barbarous cruelties. The bulls did exceedingly well, but the Irish wolf-dog exceeded, which was a tall greyhound, a stately creature indeed, who beat a cruel mastiff. One of the bulls tossed a dog full into a lady's lap, as she sat in one of the boxes at a considerable height from the arena. Two poor dogs were killed, and so all ended with the ape on horseback, and I most heartily weary of the rude and dirty pastime, which I had not seen, I think, in twenty years before." Foreigners, who have visited England in bygone times, often allude scornfully to our forefathers' barbarous diversions; but on the whole they seem rather to have enjoyed the sport. A Spanish nobleman was taken to see a poor pony baited with an ape fastened on its back; and he wrote—"to see the animal kicking amongst the dogs, with the screams of the ape, beholding the curs hanging from the ears and neck of the pony, is very laughable!" But enough has been said of these terrible and monstrous cruelties. Happily for us they no longer exist, and together with cock-fighting, throwing at cocks and hens, and other barbarous amusements, cannot now be reckoned among our sports and pastimes. It was a happy thing for us when the conscience of the nation was aroused, and the law stepped in to put an end to such disgraceful scenes which were witnessed in the Paris Garden at Southwark, or in the rude bull-run of a Yorkshire village. The Society for the Prevention of Cruelty to Animals was not known in the days of bear-baiting and cock-throwing.

CHAPTER X.

OCTOBER.

" Rivet well each coat of mail ;
Blows shall fall like showers of hail ;
Merrily the harness rings,
Of tilting lists and tournay sings,
Honour to the valiant brings.
Clink, clink, clink !"—*Armourers' Chorus.*

Tournaments—*Mysteries*—*Moralities*—*Pageants.*

IN the days of chivalry, when gallant knights used to ride about in search of adventures; and when there were many wars, battles, and crusades, martial exercises were the chief amusements of the people of England. We have already mentioned some of these sports in which the humbler folk used to show their strength and dexterity, and now I propose to tell you of those wonderful trials of military skill called tournaments, which were the favourite pastimes of the noblemen and gentry of England in the middle ages, and afforded much amusement to their poorer neighbours who flocked to see these gallant feats of arms. Tournaments were fights in miniature, in which the combatants fought simply to exhibit their strength and prowess. There was a great deal of pomp and ceremony attached to them. The lists, as the barriers were called which inclosed the scene of combat, were superbly decorated, and surrounded by pavilions belonging to the champions, ornamented with their arms and banners. The seats reserved for the noble ladies and gentlemen who came to see the fight were hung with tapestry embroidered with gold and silver. Every one was dressed in the most sumptuous manner: the minstrels and heralds were clothed in the costliest garments; the knights who were engaged in the sports and their horses were most gorgeously arrayed. The whole scene was one of great splendour and magnificence, and, when the fight began, the shouts of the heralds who directed the tournament, the clashing of arms, the clang of trumpets, the charging of the combatants, and the shouts of the spectators, must have produced a wonderfully impressive and exciting effect upon all who witnessed the strange spectacle.

The regulations and laws of the tournament were very minute. When many preliminary arrangements had been made with regard to the examination of arms and helmets and the exhibition of banners, &c., at ten o'clock on the morning of the appointed day the champions and their adherents were required to be in their places. Two cords divided the combatants, who were each armed with a pointless sword and a truncheon hanging from their saddles. When the word was given by the lord of the tournament, the cords were removed, and the champions charged and fought until the heralds sounded the signal to retire. It was considered the greatest disgrace to be unhorsed. A French earl once tried to unhorse our King Edward I. when he was returning from Palestine, wearied by the journey. The earl threw away his sword, cast his arms around the king's neck, and tried to pull him from his horse. But Edward put spurs to his horse and drew the earl from the saddle, and then shaking him violently, threw him to the ground.

The joust (or just) differed from tournament, because in the former only lances were used, and only two knights could fight at once. It was not considered quite so important as the grand feat of arms which I have just described, but was often practised when the more serious encounter had finished. Lances or spears without heads of iron were commonly used, and the object of the sport was to ride hard against one's adversary and strike him with the spear upon the front of the helmet, so as to beat him backwards from his horse, or break the spear. You will gather from these descriptions that this kind of sport was somewhat dangerous, and that men sometimes lost their lives at these encounters. In order to lessen the risk and danger of the two horses running into each other when the knights charged, a boarded

A TOURNAMENT.

railing was erected in the midst of the lists, about four or five feet high. The combatants rode on separate sides of this barrier, and therefore could not encounter each other except with their lances.

In the days of chivalry ladies were held in high honour and respect. It was their privilege to assign the prizes to those who had distinguished themselves most in the tournament. They were the arbiters of the sport; and, indeed, the jousts were usually held in honour of the ladies, who received as their right the respect and devotion of all true knights. This respect for women had a softening and ennobling influence, which was of great value in times when such influences were rare. It was probably derived (according to a French writer) from our ancestors, the Germans, "who attributed somewhat of divinity to the fair sex." It is the sign of a corrupt age and degraded manners when this respect ceases to be paid.

Only men of noble family, and who owned land, were allowed to take part in the jousts or tournament; but the yeomen and young farmers used to practise similar kinds of sport, such as tilting at a ring, quintain, and boat jousts, which have already been mentioned in a preceding chapter. Richard I., the lion-hearted king, was a great promoter of these martial sports, and appointed five places for the holding of tournaments in England, namely, at some place between Salisbury and Wilton, between Warwick and Kenilworth, between Stamford and Wallingford, between Brackley and Mixbury, and between Blie and Tykehill. But in almost every part of England tournaments or jousts have been held, and scenes enacted such as I have described. Sometimes two knights would fight in mortal combat. If one knight accused the other of crime or dishonour, the latter might challenge him to fight with swords or lances, and, according to the superstition of the times, the victor was considered to be the one who spoke the truth. But this ordeal combat was far removed from the domain of sport.

When jousts and tournaments were abandoned, tilting on horseback at a ring became a favourite courtly amusement. A ring was suspended on a level with the eye of the rider; and the sport consisted in riding towards the ring, and sending the point of a lance through it, and so bearing it away. Great skill was required to accomplish this surely and gracefully. Ascham, a writer in the sixteenth century, tells us what accomplishments were required from the complete English gentleman of the period. "To ride comely, to run fair at the tilt or ring, to play at all weapons, to shoot fair in bow, or surely in gun; to vault lustily, to run, to leap, to wrestle, to swim, to dance comely, to sing, and play of instruments cunningly; to hawk, to hunt, to play at tennis, and all pastimes generally which be joined to labour, containing either some fit exercises for war, or some pleasant pastime for peace—these be not only comely and decent, but also very necessary for a courtly gentleman to use." The courtly gentleman must have been very industrious to acquire all these numerous accomplishments!

There was another form of spectacle which gave great pleasure to our ancestors; and often in the market-places of old towns, or in open fields, at the bottom of natural amphitheatres near some of the ancient monasteries, were Scriptural plays performed, which were called *Miracles*, or *Mysteries*, because they treated of scenes taken from the Old or New Testament, or from the lives of saints and martyrs. The performances were very simple and often grotesque, but the plays were regarded by the monks, who assisted in these representations, as a means of teaching the people sacred truths. The miracle play of Norman and mediæval times was a long, disconnected performance, which often lasted many days. In the reign of Henry IV. there was a play which lasted eight days, and, beginning with the creation of the world, contained the greater part of the history of the Old and the New Testament. The words of the play seem to us strange, and sometimes profane; but they were not thought to be so by those who listened to them. The *Mystery* play only lasted one day, and consisted of one subject, such as *The Conversion of St. Paul. Noah and the Flood* was a very popular piece. His wife is represented as being much opposed to the perilous voyage in the ark, and abuses Noah very severely for compelling her to go. Sometimes the authors thought it necessary to introduce a comic character to enliven the dullness of the performance. But, in spite of humorous demons, these mysteries ceased to attract, and plays called *Moralities* were introduced, in which the actors assumed the parts of personified virtues, &c., and you might have heard "Faith" preaching to "Prudence," or "Death" lecturing "Beauty" and "Pride." The first miracle play performed in England was that of *St. Catherine*, which was acted at Dunstable, 1110 A.D.; and another early piece was the play called *The Image of St. Nicholas*. These were of a religious nature and were performed in church during Divine service. The following is an outline of the plot of the latter: instead of the image of St. Nicholas, which adorned his shrine, a man stood in the garb of the saint whom he represented. The service is divided into two portions, and the play is produced during the interval. A stranger appears at the west door, who is evidently a rich heathen, and lays down his treasures before the image of the saint and beseeches him to take care of them. A band of thieves enter and steal the treasures, and when the heathen returns, he is so enraged that he proceeds to chastise the image of the saint; when lo! the figure descends, marches out of the church, and convinces the thieves of their wickedness. Struck with fear on account of the miracle, they restore the treasures, the Pagan sings a song of joy, and St. Nicholas tells him to worship God, and to praise Christ. Then, after an act of adoration to the Almighty, the service is resumed.*

There were also strolling companies of minstrels, jugglers, and jesters, who went about the country, and acted secular pieces composed of comic stories, jokes, and dialogues, interspersed with dancing and tumbling. The whole performance was very absurd and often indecent, and the clergy did their utmost to suppress these strolling companies.

The stage upon which the *Mysteries* were played was built on wheels, in order that it might be drawn to different parts of the town. Sometimes religious plays were acted in churches before the Reformation; but in Cornwall the people formed an earthen amphitheatre in some open field, and as the players did not learn their parts very well, a prompter used to follow them about with a book and tell them what to say. Coventry, York, Wakefield, Reading, Hull, and Leicester were famous for their plays, and in the churchwardens' accounts we find many entries referring to the performances.

1469.—*e.g.*	Item paid	to Noah and his wife	xxi[d].
"	"	for a rope to hang the ship in the church	ii[d].

These performances would probably seem very foolish

* I am indebted for this description to Mr. W. Andrews' interesting book on the *Curiosities of the Church*.

and childish to a modern audience, but they helped to enliven and diversify the lives of our more simple-minded forefathers.

The people, too, loved pageants which were performed on great occasions, during a Royal progress for instance, or to welcome the advent of some mighty personage. Great preparations were made for these exhibitions of rustic talent; long verses were committed to memory; rehearsals were endless, and the stories of Greek and Roman mythology were ransacked to provide scenes and subjects for the rural pageant. All this must have afforded immense amusement and interest to the country-folk in the neighbourhood of some lord's castle, when the king or queen was expected to sojourn there. Shepherds and shepherdesses, gods and goddesses, clowns and mummers, all took part in the play, and it may interest my readers to give an account of one of these pageants, which was performed before Queen Elizabeth when she visited the ancient and historic castle of Sudeley.*

The play is founded on the old classical story of Apollo and Daphne. The sun-god, Apollo, was charmed by the beauty of the fair Daphne, the daughter of a river-god, and pursued her with base intent. Just as she was about to be overtaken she prayed for aid, and was immediately changed into a laurel-tree, which became the favourite tree of the

* Cf. *Annals of Winchcombe and Sudeley*, by Mrs. Dent.

disappointed lover. The pageant founded on this old classical legend commenced with a man, who acted the part of Apollo, chasing a woman, who represented Daphne, followed by a young shepherd bewailing his hard fate. He, too, loved the fair and beautiful Daphne, but Apollo wooed her with fair words, and threatened him with diverse penalties, saying he would change him into a wolf, or a cockatrice, or blind his eyes. The shepherd in a long speech tells how Daphne was changed into a tree, and then Apollo is seen at the foot of a laurel-tree weeping, accompanied by two minstrels. The repentant god repeats the verse—

"Sing you, play you; but sing and play my truth;
This tree my lute, these sighs my note of ruth:
The laurel leaf for ever shall be green,
And Chastity shall be Apollo's Queen.
If gods may die, here shall my tomb be placed,
And this engraven, 'Fond Phœbus, Daphne chaste.'"

A song follows, and then, wonderful to relate, the tree opens, and Daphne comes forth. Apollo resigns her to the humble shepherd, and then she runs to her Majesty the Queen, and with a great deal of flattery wishes her a long and prosperous reign.

Such was the simple play which delighted the minds of our forefathers, and helped to raise them from sordid cares and the dull monotony of continual toil. In our popular amusements the village folk do not take part, except as spectators, and therefore lose half the pleasure; whereas in the time of the Virgin Queen the rehearsals, the learning the speeches by heart, the dresses, the excitement, all contributed to give them fresh ideas and new thoughts. The acting may not have been very good; indeed Queen Elizabeth did not always think very highly of the performances of her subjects at Coventry, and was heard to exclaim, "What fools ye Coventry folk are!" but I think her Majesty must have been pleased at the concluding address of the players at Sudeley. After the shepherds had acted a piece in which the election of the King and Queen of the Bean formed a part, they knelt before the real Queen, and said, "Pardon, dread Sovereign, poor shepherds' pastimes, and bold shepherds' presumptions. We call ourselves kings and queens to make mirth; but when we see a king or queen, we stand amazed. At chess there are kings and queens, and they of wood. Shepherds are no more, nor no less, wooden. In theatres workmen have played emperors; yet the next day forgotten neither their duties nor occupation. For our boldness in borrowing their names, and in not seeing your Majesty for our blindness, we offer these shepherds' weeds: which, if your Majesty vouchsafe at any time to wear, it shall bring to our hearts comfort, and happiness to our labours."

When the Queen visited Kenilworth Castle, splendid pageants were performed in her honour. As she entered the castle the gigantic porter recited verses to greet her Majesty, gods and goddesses offered gifts and compliments on bended knee, and the Lady of the Lake, surrounded by Tritons and Nereids, came on a floating island to do homage to the peerless Elizabeth, and to welcome her to all the sport the castle could afford. For an account of the strange conduct of Orion and his dolphin upon this occasion, we refer our readers to Sir Walter Scott's *Kenilworth*, and the lover of pageants will find much to interest him in Gascoigne's *Princely Progress*. In many of the chief towns of England the members of the Guilds were obliged by their ordinances to have a pageant once every year, which was of a religious nature. The Guild of St. Mary at Beverley made a yearly representation of the Presentation of Christ in the Temple, one of their number being dressed as a queen to represent the Virgin, "having what may seem a son in her arms," two others representing Joseph and Simeon, and two others going as angels carrying lights. The people of England seem always to have had a great fondness for shows and pageants.

CHAPTER XI.

NOVEMBER.

"The ploughman, though he labour hard,
Yet on the holiday
Heigh trolollie, lollie loe.
No emperor so merrily
Doth pass his time away;
Then care away,
And wend along with me."—*Complete Angler.*

"The curious preciseness,
And all pretended gravity of those
That seek to banish hence these harmless sports,
Have thrust away much ancient honesty."—IRVING'S *Sketch Book.*

All-hallow Eve—"Soul Cakes"—Diving for Apples—The Fifth of November—Martinmas—*Demands Joyous*—Indoor Games.

THE first of November is All Saints' Day, and the eve of that day, called All-hallow Even, was the occasion of some very ancient and curious customs. It seems to have been observed more by the descendants of the Celts than by the Saxons; and Wales, Scotland, and Ireland were the homes of many of the popular superstitions connected with this festival. In Scotland the bonfires were set up in every village, and each member of a family would throw in a white stone marked with his name ; and if that stone could not be found next morning, it was supposed that that person would die before the following All Saints' Day. This foolish superstition may be classed with the other well-known superstition with regard to the sitting of thirteen people at one table, in which some are still foolish enough to believe.

All-hallow Even was supposed to be a great night for witches : possibly it was with the intention of guarding against their spells that the farmers used to carry blazing straw around their cornfields and stacks. It was the custom for the farmer to regale his men with seed cake on this night ; and there were cakes called "Soul Mass Cakes," or "Soul Cakes," which were given to the poor. These were of triangular shape, and poor people in Staffordshire used to go *a-souling*, i. e. collecting these soul cakes, or anything else they could get.

On this night the fishermen of Scotland signed their boats, that is put a cross of tar upon them, in order that their fishing might prosper. The church bells were rung all night long for all Christian souls, and we find from some old account books that the good folk were very careful to have all their bell-ropes and bells in good order for All-hallow Even. This ringing was supposed to benefit the souls of the dead in Purgatory, and was suppressed after the Reformation.

There were some very homely pastimes for All-hallow Even for the young folk in the north of England. Apples were placed in a vessel of water and "dived for"; or they were suspended from the roof and caught at by several expectant mouths. Sometimes a rod was suspended with an apple at one end, and at the other a lighted candle. The youths had their hands tied behind their backs, and caught at the apple, often causing the candle to swing round and burn their hair. The cracking of nuts was an important ceremony among the young men and maidens, who threw nuts into the fire, and from the way in which they cracked, or burned, foretold all kinds of happiness or misery for themselves. The nuts that burned brightly prophesied prosperity to their owners, but those that crackled or burned black denoted misfortune. In olden times, when people were more superstitious than they are now, they attached great importance to these omens and customs, but happily the young people of our times have ceased to believe in magic and foolish customs, and country girls strive to attract their swains by other charms than those of nut-cracking on All-hallow Even.

We have still our bonfires on November 5th, but the event which happened on that day is very recent as compared with many of the old customs of which I have been writing. However, it is nearly three hundred years ago since Guy Fawkes and his companions attempted to blow up the Houses of Parliament with gunpowder; and yet we still light our bonfires and burn Guy Fawkes' effigy, with much accompaniment of squibs and crackers, just as if the event which we commemorate only occurred last year. Probably very few of our rustics think much of the origin of the customs observed on November the Fifth, or remember that it was instituted by the House of Commons as "a holiday for ever in thankfulness to God for our deliverance, and detestation of the Papists;" but this ignorance does not prevent them from keeping up the custom and enjoying the excitement of the bonfire and fireworks. If you are not acquainted with the history of the conspiracy, I would advise you to read it in some good history book, and—

"Pray to remember
The fifth of November
Gunpowder treason and plot,
When the King and his train
Had nearly been slain,
Therefore it shall not be forgot."

The Berkshire boys, as they carried their Guy and collected wood for their bonfires, used to add the words—

"Our king's a valiant soldier,
With his blunderbuss on his shoulder,
Cocks his pistol, draws his rapier;
Pray give us something for his sake here.
A stick and a stake, for our good king's sake:
If ye won't give one, I'll take two,
The better for me, and the worse for you.

CHORUS—

"Hollow, boys, hollow, boys, make the bells ring,
Hollow, boys, hollow, boys, God save the King."

Some of the rhymes tell us about the nefarious deeds of wicked Guy Fawkes, who

". . . with his companions did contrive
To blow the House of Parliament up alive,
With three score barrels of powder down below,
To prove Old England's wicked overthrow;
But by God's mercy all of them got catched,
With their dark lantern, and their lighted match.
Ladies and gentlemen sitting by the fire,
Please put hands in pockets and give us our desire:
While you can drink one glass, we can drink two,
The better for we, and none the worse for you."

This rhyme was concluded with the following strange jingle—

"Rumour, rumour, pump a derry,
Prick his heart and burn his body,
And send his soul to Purgatory." *

The streets of Oxford used to be the scenes of great encounters between the townsmen and gownsmen (or college students) on this night, who, on any other night in the year, never thought of fighting. Happily in recent years these fights have ceased, but even now the gownsmen are "gated" on the night of the Fifth of November, *i.e.* are confined to their colleges, lest there should be a renewal of these

* Cf. *Glossary of Berkshire Words and Phrases*, by Major B. Lowsley, R.E.

encounters. So severe were the battles in ancient times, that the tower of Carfax Church was lowered because the townsfolk used to ascend thither and shoot their arrows at the undergraduates; and the butchers were obliged to ply their trade beyond the city walls, because they had used their knives and cleavers in their annual fight.

At Martinmas, or the Feast of St. Martin, it was the custom to lay in a stock of winter provisions, and many cows, oxen, and swine were killed at this time, their flesh being salted and hung up for the winter, when fresh provisions were seldom to be had.

And now the long evenings have set in, and our ancestors in hall or cottage assemble round the blazing hearth, and listen to the minstrel's lays, and recite their oft-told tales of adventure and romance. Sometimes they indulge in asking each other riddles, and there exists at the present time an old collection of these early efforts of wit and humour which are not of a very high order. The book is called *Demands Joyous*, and was printed in A.D. 1511. I may extract the following riddles:—"What is it that never was and never will be? Answer: A mouse's nest in a cat's ear. Why does a cow lie down? Because it cannot sit. How many straws go to a goose's nest? Not one, for straws, not having feet, cannot go anywhere."

With such feeble efforts of wit did the country folk try to beguile the long evenings. In those days there were no newspapers, very few books, even if they could be read, and the only means of gathering information from other parts of the country were the peddlers or wandering minstrels, who told them the news as they passed from place to place. Consequently, the above humble efforts of wit were not to be despised, and served to beguile the tediousness of the long winter's night. Besides, the villagers had the carols to practise for Christmas, many of which were handed down from father to son for many generations, and probably both words and music received many variations in their course. Old collections of these carols still exist, such as the one entitled, "Good and True, Fresh and New, Christmas Carols," which was made in the middle of the seventeenth century. As an instance of the way in which the words became changed as they were passed on by illiterate singers, I may mention a carol of which the refrain is now printed "Now Well, Now Well"; originally this must have been "Noel, Noel." Some of the carols degenerated into songs about the wassail bowl, and the virtues of strong ale, and our forefathers were not unlike some of their children, who forget the Saviour in the enjoyment of His gifts. And besides the carols the villagers had the ordinary hymns to practise, with grand accompaniment of violins, flutes, clarionets, etc., for each village had its own musicians, who took great pride and interest in their playing, and used to practise together in the evenings. The old instruments have vanished: we have our organs and harmoniums: our choirs sing better and more reverently; but there are no reunions of the village orchestra, which used to afford so much pleasure to the rustics of former days.

In the lord's hall there were plenty of sedentary games, and amongst these pre-eminently stands the noble pastime of chess. It is very ancient, and is supposed to have been invented by Xerxes, a philosopher in the court of Evil-Merodach, king of Babylon. It was well known in England before the Conquest, and Canute was very fond of the chessboard. King John was so engrossed in this game that when some messengers came to tell him that the French king had besieged one of his cities, he would not listen to them until he had finished his chess. The complicated movements of the various men seem to show that the game was developed and improved, and not the invention of one man, but few changes have been made during several centuries. Players are checkmated now in very much the same way as they were five hundred years ago.

Besides chess they had backgammon, or tables, as the game was called, Merelles, or Nine men's Morris (which also found its way to the shepherds' cottages), dice, and card games, some of which I have described before. Gambling was often carried on to a great extent, but evidently our modern people are not wiser than their ancestors in this matter; and instead of playing games for recreation, are not satisfied until they lose fortunes on the hazard of a dice or a card. Let us hope that men will at length become wiser as the world grows older.

Erasmus, the learned Dutchman, in his *Colloquies* suggests some curious awards for victors. He represents two youths, Adolphus and Bernard, who begin to play a game at bowls. Adolphus says, "What shall he that beats get, or he that is beaten lose?" Bernard replies, "What if he that beats shall have a piece of his ear cut off? It is a mean thing to play for money: you are a German, and I a Frenchman: we will both play for the honour of his country. If I shall beat you, you shall cry out thrice, 'Let France flourish!' if I shall be beat (which I hope I shall not), I will in the same words celebrate your Germany." They bowl away: a stone represents the Jack: a mischievous bit of brickbat rather interferes with the German's accuracy of aim, but in the end he wins, and the French cock has to crow thrice, "Let Germany flourish." In another game between two students who are contending in the play of striking a ball through an iron ring, it is arranged that he that is beat shall make and repeat extempore some verses in praise of him that beat him. This certainly would make many a youth keen to win the contest!

CHAPTER XII.

DECEMBER.

> "The Darling of the world is come,
> And fit it is we find a room
> To welcome Him. The nobler part
> Of all the house here is the heart,
>
> "Which we will give Him; and bequeath
> This holly and this ivy wreath
> To do Him honour, who's our King,
> And Lord of all this revelling."
>
> HERRICK, *A Christmas Carol.*

St. Nicholas Day—The Boy Bishop—Christmas Eve—Christmas Customs—Mummers—"Lord of Misrule"—Conclusion.

NOW dark and chill December has arrived; and very dark and chill it must have seemed to our ancestors. No gaslights illuminated the streets, here and there a feeble oil lamp helped to make the darkness visible, when the oil was not frozen: the roads were deep with mud, and everything outside was cold and cheerless. But within the farmer's kitchen the huge logs burned brightly, and the Christmas holidays were at hand with the accustomed merrymakings, to cheer the hearts of all in the depths of the dreary winter.

But before Christmas Day arrived, the children enjoyed a great treat on St. Nicholas' Day, December 6th, when it was the custom for parents to convey secretly presents of various kinds to their little sons and daughters, who were taught to believe that they owed them to the kindness of St. Nicholas, who, going up and down among the towns and villages, came in at the windows and distributed the gifts. St. Nicholas, who died A.D. 343, threw a purse filled with money into the bedroom of a poor man for the benefit of his three daughters, who were in sore trouble; and this story seems to have originated the custom which has been observed in many countries, and brought much enjoyment to the young folk who received St. Nicholas' bounty.

Before the Reformation there was another very strange custom associated with this day; namely, the election of a boy bishop, who was dressed in episcopal robes, with a mitre on his head, and who actually was allowed to preach in the church. This was done regularly at many of our cathedrals and collegiate churches, and we find records of the custom amongst the archives of Salisbury and many other places; even the service which they used is in existence. The youthful bishop was elected by the choir-boys, and exercised his functions until Holy Innocents' Day. On that day in great state he entered the cathedral surrounded by the other boys, who played the part of prebendaries, and attended by the dean and canons, who on this occasion yielded up their dignity to the youthful prelate and his followers. The collect for Holy Innocents' Day in our Prayer-book formed part of the service. It was a strange ceremony, not unmixed with irreverence, and happily has long been discontinued, being forbidden by Royal proclamation in 1542, and finally abolished by Elizabeth.

In the archives of the ancient town of Bristol there is a book of directions for the Mayor and his brethren, and on St. Nicholas' Day they are ordered to go to the Church of St. Nicholas and join in the festival of the boy bishop, to hear his sermon and receive his blessing. Then they dined together, and waited for the young bishop to come to them, playing the meanwhile at dice, the town clerk being ordered to find the dice, and to receive a penny for every raffle. The bishop was regaled with bread and wine, and preached again to the Mayor and corporation in the evening. I am informed that a curious memorial of this custom existed until recent years in one village at least. An old lady recollected that when she was a child she was allowed to play with her companions in church on St. Nicholas' Day.

But Christmas is approaching, and we must hasten to describe that bright and happy festival. The holiday began on Christmas Eve, and perhaps you have wondered why we hang up mistletoe, and decorate our churches and houses with holly, why our ancestors brought in the Yule-log, and performed many other customs which do not seem to be very closely connected with the celebration of the birthday of our Lord. But we must remember that our forefathers were originally heathen, and at this period of the year they practised several strange customs connected with their Druidical worship, and held great feasts in honour of their gods. When Christian missionaries converted these heathen, they strove to put down some of the old idolatrous practices; but their efforts were in vain, for the people were warmly attached to these old rights and usages. So a compromise was effected: the old Pagan customs were shorn of their idolatry and transferred to our Christian festivals. Cutting the mistletoe was distinctly a rite practised by the Druids, who cut the sacred plant with a golden knife, and sacrificed two white bulls to the sylvan deities whom they thus sought to propitiate. We hang up our bunches of mistletoe now, but we do not attach any superstitious importance to it, nor imagine that any gods of the woods will be influenced by our procedure. The bringing in of the Yule-log was a Norse custom observed in honour of Thor, from whose name we derive our word Thursday or Thor's-day. The mighty log was drawn into the baronial hall with great pomp, while the bards sang their songs of praise and chanted "Welcome Yule."

"Welcome be Thou, heavenly King,
Welcome, born on this morning;
Welcome for whom we shall sing
Welcome, Yule."

Herrick, who delighted so much in singing of

"Maypoles, hock-carts, wassails, wakes—"

then bursts out in joyous strains:

"Come, bring with a noise,
My merry, merry boys,
The Christmas log to the firing;
While my good dame, she
Bids ye all be free
And drink to your heart's desiring.
With the last year's brand
Light the new block, and
For good success in his spending,
On your psaltries play,
That sweet luck may
Come while the log is a-teending."

We can fancy that we see the ceremony, the glad procession of retainers and servants, the lights flaring in all directions: we can hear the shouts and chorus of many voices, the drums beating and flutes and trumpets sounding. The huge hearth receives the mighty log, and the flames and sparks shoot up the gaping chimney.

At Court in olden times Christmas was kept right royally, if we may judge from the extensive *menu* of the repasts of King Henry III. and his courtiers in the year 1247. He kept his Christmas at Winchester Castle, and the neighbourhood must have been ransacked to furnish supplies for the royal table. The choice dainties were as follows: Boars, with heads entire, well cooked and very succulent, 48; fowls, 1900; partridges, mostly "put in paste," 500; swans, 41; peacocks, 48; hares, 260; eggs, 24,000; 300 gallons of oysters; 300 rabbits, and more if possible; birds of various sorts, as many as could be had; of whitings, "particularly good and heavy," and conger eels the same; a hundred mullets, "fat and very heavy." For bread the king paid £27 10*s*., at the price of four loaves to the penny. When the king kept his Christmas at York in 1250, the royal treasury must have been very full, for he ordered for the royal banquets 7000 fowls, 1750 partridges, besides immense numbers of boars, swans, pheasants, &c. Of course the king had a very large retinue of vassals and feudal lords to provide for; but the store seems sufficiently vast to supply the wants of an army of faithful, but hungry, subjects. Sometimes, when the king was short of money, there was a considerable reduction in the amount of good things consumed at Christmas.

Our ancestors were very careful to attend the services of the church, which their loving hands had adorned with holly, bay, rosemary, and laurel. They considered it a day of special thanksgiving and rejoicing, as an old poet observed—

> "At Christmas be merry and thankful with all,
> And feast thy poor neighbours, the great and the small."

The solemn service of Holy Communion was celebrated on Christmas Eve, in mediæval times—the only night in all the year when an evening celebration was allowed. The halls of the knights and barons of ancient days were thrown open to all comers, and open house was kept for a fortnight. Rejoicing at Christmas time seems to have been universal, and it is not for us to judge whether in their mirth they sometimes forgot the reason of true Christmas joy, and thought more of their feasting than of Him who was born on Christmas Day. But by their hearty manner of keeping this annual festival, by the hospitality which the farmers and rich men showed to their labourers and poorer neighbours, they promoted, at any rate, "goodwill amongst men"—old animosities, quarrels, and bitternesses were forgotten, and the hearts of the poor cheered.

In the North of England every farmer gave two feasts, one called "the old folks' night," and the other "the young folks' night." The old Squire used to receive his tenants and neighbours at daybreak, when the black-jacks were passed round, and woe betide the luckless cook who had overslept herself, and had not boiled the Hackin, or large sausage, ere the day dawned, for then she was seized by the arms and made to run round the market-place, or courtyard, until she was ashamed of her laziness.

And now let us enter the hall of some great baron and see how our ancestors kept a merry Christmas. The panelled walls, and stags' horns, and gallery at one end of the great room were hung with holly and mistletoe. The Yule-log blazed upon the hearth, and then entered the vassals, tenants, and servants of the lord to share in the Christmas banquet. Rank and ceremony were laid aside: all were deemed equal, whether lords or barons, serfs or peasants—a custom which arose, doubtless, from the remembrance of Him who on the first Christmas Day, "although He was rich, yet for our sakes became poor."

And now on the huge oaken table were placed the various dishes of the feast—a mighty boar's head, decorated with laurel and rosemary, whose approach was often heralded with trumpets as the king of the feast; then came a peacock, stuffed with spices and sweet herbs, and adorned with its gay feathers, and then followed a goodly company of geese, capons, sirloins of beef, pheasants, mince-pies, and plum-porridge. A carol was often sung when the boar's head was brought in; here is one from the collection of Wynkyn de Worde:

> Caput Apri defero
> Reddens laudes Domino,
> The Boar's Head in hand bring I
> With garlands gay and rosemary;
> I pray you all sing merrily
> Qui estis in convivio.
>
> The Boar's Head, I understand,
> Is the chief service in this land;
> Look wherever it be fande:
> Servite cum cantico.
>
> Be glad, lords, both more and lasse,
> For this hath ordained our stewárd
> To cheer you all this Christmasse,
> The Boar's Head with mustárd.*

Neither were the ale and wassail-bowl forgotten, and they circulated sometimes too often, I fear, and laid the seeds of gout and other evils, from which other generations suffer. But when the prodigious appetites of the company had been appeased, the maskers and

* The custom of bringing in the boar's head is still preserved at Queen's College, Oxford. The story is told of a student of the college who was attacked by a wild boar while he was diligently studying Aristotle during a walk near Shotover Hill. His book was his only means of defence, so he thrust the volume down the animal's throat, exclaiming, "It is Greek!" The boar found Greek very difficult to digest, and died on the spot, and the head was brought home in triumph by the student. Ever since that date, for five hundred years, a boar's head has graced the college table at Christmas.

mummers entered the hall and performed strange antics and a curious play, fragments of which have come down to our own time. The youths of the villages of England still come round at Christmas-time and act their mumming-drama, in which "St. George" kills a "Turkish knight," who is raised to life by "Medicine Man," and performs a very important part of the play—passing round the money-box. This is a remnant of the mumming of ancient days, and perhaps of some "mystery" play, of which I told you in a previous chapter.

In Berkshire the characters are represented by "Molly," a stalwart man dressed in a woman's gown, shawl, and bonnet, with a besom in his hand, who strives in his dialogue to imitate a woman's voice; King George, a big burly man dressed as a knight, with a wooden sword and a home-made helmet; a French officer, with a cocked hat and sword; a Doctor, who wears a pig-tail; Jack Vinny, a jester; Happy Jack, a humorous character dressed in tattered garments, and Old Beelzebub, who appears as Father Christmas. In some parts of the royal county the part of King George is taken by an "Africky king," and a Turkish knight instead of the French officer. Very curious are the words of the old play, and very ludicrous the representation when the parts are acted by competent players.

There was also in the baron's hall a great person dressed in a very fantastic garb, who was here, there, and everywhere, directing the mummers, making jokes to amuse the company, and looking after everybody. He was called the "Lord of Misrule." Sometimes his rule was harmless enough, and did good service in directing the revels; but often he was more worthy of his name, and was guilty of all kinds of absurd and mischievous pranks, which did great harm, and were very profane. But these were not part of the Christmas feast, where all was happiness and mirth. Sir Walter Scott says, in his description of the festival—

> "England was merry England when
> Old Christmas brought his sports again;
> A Christmas gambol oft would cheer
> A poor man's heart through all the year."

All the old poets sing in praise of the great day which, as Herrick says, "sees December turned to May," and which makes the "chilling winter's morn smile like a field beset with corn." Old carols chant in reverent strains their homage to the infant Saviour: some reflect time-honoured customs and social joys when old age casts aside its solemnity and mingles once more in the light-hearted gaiety of youth, and all unite in chanting the praises of this happy festival. The poet Withers sings—

> "Lo! now is come our joyful'st feast!
> Let every man be jolly;
> Each room with ivy leaves is drest,
> And every post with holly.

"Now all our neighbours' chimneys smoke,
And Christmas blocks are burning;
Their ovens they with baked meats choke,
And all their spits are turning.

"Without the door let sorrow lie,
And if, for cold, it has to die,
We'll bury it in Christmas pie,
And evermore be merry."

Thus the happy night was spent; and if, like grave elders, we look down upon these frolics of a younger age, and think ourselves so much wiser and better than our forefathers, we should not forget the benefits which come from open-handed hospitality, goodwill, and simple manners, nor scornfully regard honest merriment and light-hearted gaiety. A light heart is generally not far removed from a holy heart.

Yes, England was merry England then; and although there were plenty of troubles in those days, when plagues decimated whole villages, when wars were frequent, food scarce, and oppression common, yet the Christmas festivities, the varieties of sports and pastimes which each season provided, the homely customs and bonds of union between class and class which these observances strengthened, added brightness to the lives of our simple forefathers, who might otherwise have sunk beneath the burdens of their daily toil. We have seen how many customs and sports, which were at first simple and harmless, degenerated and were abused: we have noticed some of the bad features of these ancient pastimes, such as cruelty to animals and intemperance; and are thankful that there is some improvement manifest in these respects. But it is interesting to witness again in imagination the scenes that once took place in our market-places and on our village greens; and, if it be impossible to restore again the glories of May Day and the brightness of the Christmas feast, we may still find plenty of harmless and innocent recreation, and learn to be merry, and at the same time wise.

INDEX.

THE END.

Richard Clay & Sons, Limited, London & Bungay.